Southern Spirit

A MAX PORTER PARANORMAL MYSTERY

Stuart Jaffe

Southern Spirit is a work of fiction. Names, characters, places, and incidents either are the product of the author's imagination or are used fictitiously, and any resemblance to any persons, living or dead, business establishments, events, or locales is entirely coincidental.

SOUTHERN SPIRIT

Cover art by Claudia Ianniciello

ISBN 13: 978-1-963517-02-6

First Edition: November, 2017
First Hardcover Edition: February, 2024

For Eddie, Boom,
Buffy, and Kai

Also by Stuart Jaffe

Max Porter Paranormal Mysteries

Southern Bound
Southern Charm
Southern Belle
Southern Gothic
Southern Haunts
Southern Curses
Southern Rites
Southern Craft
Southern Spirit
Southern Flames
Southern Fury
Southern Souls
Southern Blood
Southern Graves
Southern Dead
Southern Hexes
Southern Hart

Nathan K Thrillers

Immortal Killers
Killing Machine
The Cardinal
Yukon Massacre
The First Battle
Immortal Darkness
A Spy for Eternity
Prisoner
Desert Takedown
Lone Star Standoff
The Puppeteer
Blowback
Prime

The Ridnight Mysteries

The Water Blade
The Waters of Taladoro
Waterfire

The Parallel Society

The Infinity Caverns
Book on the Isle
Rift Angel
Lost Time
Pages of Glass
The Bold Warrior
City of Infinity

The Malja Chronicles

The Way of the Black Beast
The Way of the Sword and Gun
The Way of the Brother Gods
The Way of the Blade
The Way of the Power
The Way of the Soul

Gillian Boone novels

A Glimpse of Her Soul
Pathway to Spirit

Stand Alone Novels

After The Crash
Real Magic
Founders

Short Story Collection

10 Bits of My Brain
10 More Bits of My Brain
The Bluesman
The Marshall Drummond Case Files: Cabinet 1
The Marshall Drummond Case Files: Cabinet 2
The Marshall Drummond Case Files: Cabinet 3

Non-Fiction

How to Write Magical Words: A Writer's Companion
For more information, please visit ***www.stuartjaffe.com***

Southern Spirit

Chapter 1

MAX PORTER'S KNEE BOUNCED LIKE A JACKHAMMER until Sandra placed a hand on his leg. His wife threw a stern look his way, one that warned him to calm down or deal with her wrath. But beneath her harsh glare, he saw understanding — after all, never before had they sat in a living room belonging to a coven of witches.

In fact, the entire house belonged to the Mobley Coven, also known as the Coven of the Carolinas — one of the most powerful covens in the South that prided itself on keeping a low profile while simultaneously defying any who tried to hold power over them, such as the Hull family once did. This all according to the private witch-wiki Sandra knew about. That, of course, only added to Max's nerves. Sandra's knowledge of witchcraft had grown at an astounding rate.

Once Max had backed off his objections, she devoured every book she could find, she pored over websites, she joined forums, and she became the Porter Agency's *de facto* expert. It should not have come as a surprise that the witch community took notice, but Max did feel sucker-punched when earlier that day Sandra walked into the office to announce the Mobley Coven had reached out to her. They wanted to talk about something vital.

The rough voice of Marshall Drummond, their partner and a ghost of a detective from the 1940s, burst in, "How much longer do we have to wait here? They're the ones who said this was so important we had to rush on down here. So, what's the holdup?"

Sandra turned her strong eyes onto the ghost — while Max had only ever been able to see Drummond, Sandra could see all ghosts, including Drummond. "We've been here less than ten minutes. Have some patience."

"You two might have to sit there all polite, but I don't. I'm checking this place out. Maybe I'll find something interesting like a secret room." The ghost tightened his trench coat and lowered his Fedora as if bracing against a harsh storm. Then he slipped through the living room walls.

Nice walls, Max thought. Not just the walls, but the entire house looked well-cared for. If not for the fact that he knew the house belonged to a coven, he would easily have assumed a classic, all-American-type family owned the place. Nestled in the back corner of a mid-priced development, nothing about it suggested the use of spells. No odd odors, no strange sounds. And no secret rooms — at least, none that they had seen so far.

But Max admitted that they had not seen much of the house. They had driven south out of downtown Winston-Salem and came upon the development just off Darwick Road. The lawn had been freshly mowed and a minivan sat in the driveway. When they rang the doorbell, a young lady with a soft face answered and sat them in the living room.

All too normal.

"I knew it," Drummond said as he floated back into the living room. "Everything about the place looks normal except there's a room on the second floor that I can't get into — it's been warded against ghosts."

Max's gut tightened. Suddenly, the light curtains, the plush couch, the thick carpeting, the cute knick-knacks, and the warm paintings became fictions of a home. He could sense the cold of witchcraft seeping through the wood. They should never have come here. This was a bad idea all around.

"Hon," Max said and placed his hand over hers. "We should probably go."

"Stop it," she said. "Both of you. Show a little respect. They went out of their way to contact me, so let's at least hear them out."

"Because hearing out witches always goes so well," he said, absently rubbing his chest. The curse branded into him by Mother Hope, leader of the powerful Magi, heated up whenever he thought about it. She had agreed never to use it against him as long as he behaved — making it a grenade she could pull the pin out of whenever she felt like it. "I'm not comfortable with this. I know you're better about the witches and all, but let's go now. We can talk to them on the phone or—"

A middle-aged woman entered the living room carrying a serving tray with a carafe of coffee and three china cups. "I apologize for the wait," she said. Her voice played into the suburban facade surrounding them as did the simple skirt and blouse that she wore. She set the tray down and served the coffee. "Being a bunch of witches, you'd think we would have some way to make coffee faster, but alas. And don't get me started on those instant cup things. Not for me. Call me old fashioned, but sometimes the old ways are the best."

"And what *should* we call you?" Sandra asked.

"My apologies, again. I'm Lena Mobley."

After handing Max and Sandra each a cup, she settled in a high-backed, upholstered chair and sipped her coffee. Despite her stark, black hair and dangerous, red lipstick, her attitude seemed friendly, almost welcoming. Max, though, had no intention of consuming anything offered him by a witch, but he also had no desire to insult the woman. He set the cup back on the serving tray and made a show of pulling out his notepad — as if his eagerness to help the woman surpassed his manners.

"Please," he said, leaning his elbows on his knees, "tell us what we can do for you."

"Oh, I'm not sure *you* can do much at all. But your darling wife, she might be able to help. At least, I hope so."

Before Max could snap out a witty reply, Sandra said, "We're a package deal. When you hire the Porter Agency, you get all of us."

"Of course," Lena said.

The lady that had answered the door entered the room. Getting a better look at her, Max saw a college girl with a ponytail and a naive smile. In the time since she had escorted them to wait in the living room, the young lady had gone off somewhere and changed her outfit. In another setting, Max would have thought she had dressed up for a college costume party — long black gown with black lace covering her shoulders and neck — but in this house, she might wear such things all the time.

Lena put out her hand until the young lady sat on the arm of the chair. "This is my sister, Jessica. You'll have to forgive me for not bringing the rest of the sisters out to greet you, but they are all off searching."

"Searching?" Sandra said.

"That's why you're here. One of our coven has gone missing."

Jessica sniffled and produced a black handkerchief from an unseen pocket. Max couldn't tell if the tears were genuine or forced, but he knew Lena's concern rang true. Yet she had played the calm and gracious host until now.

Drummond floated near the corner of the ceiling with his arms crossed. "Just reminding you two that we are in a coven's home and they've got a room warded against us. I'm voting we leave this place before we hear anything we can't unhear."

Max agreed. "I'm sorry that you've lost one of your group, but that's really a matter for the police. You should file a Missing Persons report."

Lena's gentle grin vanished. "I should think it's obvious that our kind cannot go to the police. Certainly not for something as delicate as this."

"Why is it delicate? A person's gone missing."

"And here I thought you were a smart man. The police are not interested in an adult missing for only twenty-four hours. And we'd rather not bring their scrutiny into our world."

"The police don't need to know about covens and witches to search for a person."

Before Lena could react — and to Max's mind, that reaction looked rather angry — Sandra set her coffee down with a clink. "Please forgive my husband. He doesn't mean to be rude, but he also doesn't know the subtleties of a coven. If you would, please, tell us as much as you can about what happened."

Lena and Jessica exchanged an inscrutable look. "Her name is Laverne Mobley. She is a bit older than myself. One of the most loved and cherished of our coven. Well, yesterday morning the weekly income needed to be deposited at the bank and —"

"Weekly income?" Max said. "From what?"

Making no effort to hide her annoyance at the interruption, she said, "We have a small store that sells ingredients necessary to our work. We also fulfill online orders, but the bulk of our income is in the form of services."

Sandra patted Max's leg. "They perform spells upon request."

"I understood fine," Max said.

"We do all kinds of spells," Lena went on. "For the general public, it's mostly harmless or useless things — luck charms or love potions. Minor and inconsequential. For those in the real community, we do more serious spells but never anything dangerous."

Drummond snickered. "Sure. I bet they're squeaky clean."

"Anyway, Laverne offered to take in the money and she headed out to the bank. After she made the deposit, she said she went to the pharmacy. And that was it. She never returned. She never phoned or texted again. Nothing."

"So you called us right away?" Max asked. The whole thing sounded off.

"The first thing we did was to cast a basic location spell. That turned up nothing which could mean she's been taken out of range or perhaps whoever stole her has used magic to block our spell. There are numerous other possibilities. Your wife knows. She can explain it to you later."

"I'll remember that. What else did you try? Did you summon something to find her? A ghost, perhaps?"

"Hey," Drummond said. "Don't be giving them ideas."

Jessica put her hand on Lena's shoulder, and Max got the distinct impression that the touch had been meant to calm Lena. A breath later, Lena said, "We performed all the proper spells expected in this situation without resorting to dangerous things such as you suggest. We want to hire your agency to find her. If you fail, then perhaps we'll consider more risky behavior."

Sandra said, "Did Laverne have any enemies? Did somebody threaten her recently?"

Lena grinned. "We're witches. Of course, we had enemies. We get threatened all the time. However, I must admit that recently we've been in a more sensitive state. Our enemies have grown bolder and their reasons may not be so pure."

Biting back his frustration, Max said, "That's quite vague. If you want us to be able to help, we need more specifics."

"I'm afraid that's all I can really say. If it helps, she went to the Triad Pharmacy on Waughtown Street."

Drummond smacked his hands together to get some attention. "Will you two stop asking pointless questions? Let's get out of here. It's not like you're actually considering taking their case."

Brushing at his pants, Max stood. They had come as requested, they had listened, and now they needed to go. But Sandra did not move. The witches took notice, and an unsettling quiet came over the room. It took a bit of his will to remain standing.

"I understand," Lena finally said as she pulled a checkbook from her pocket. "I had hoped that we would convince you to help us out of respect." Looking at Sandra, she said, "Particularly you. But, as you said, the two of you are a team. I have no doubt that Mr. Porter would rather not work for a witch coven. So, I shall appeal to your more base instincts." Ripping loose a check, she held the paper out to Max. "We took the liberty of investigating your business a little bit. Jessica here is quite capable with a computer. While she has made it clear that our estimate is rough, it doesn't matter since our offer is to approximate your yearly income."

Max snatched the check far quicker than he had intended. Their research hit the mark quite close. Though loathe to admit it, he found the money tempting. Business had not been bad of late, but they had learned the crucial first rule in the life of self-employment — nothing remained constant. One month business would be booming. The next month — crickets. The idea of getting paid a full year's salary for one job meant food on the table, house and car upkeep maintained, and maybe even some financial breathing room.

Sandra must have known all the thoughts that raced through his head because she did not say a word. She sat there with her hands in her lap and looked up at him. Max could read her face well. She knew the conclusion already and merely waited for him to catch up.

"You're kidding me," Drummond said, clearly catching on as well.

Pocketing the check, Max turned to Lena and put out his hand. "Looks like we're working for a witch coven."

Chapter 2

MAX ENTERED THEIR DOWNTOWN OFFICE and settled at his desk. Sandra flicked on the lights as she came in behind. Neither had spoken on the drive back, and Drummond had been notably absent. Rubbing his face, Max prepared for somebody to be ticked off.

"Oh, you're finally back," Drummond said, poking his head out of the built-in bookcase.

Max's stomach rumbled. They had skipped breakfast, and he could smell the alluring aroma of lunchtime cooking drifting up from the corner shop nearby. To keep his mind off food and Drummond, Max pulled out a photograph of Laverne that the coven had provided. She looked about mid-fifties, thick, red hair, and a devilish grin that made her chosen endeavor entirely believable. If Max hadn't known already, he would have guessed he looked at a witch.

"I've got something to say." Drummond swept into the center of the office, his hands snapping out as he spouted his exasperation. "It's become undeniable that the two of you like to ignore me when it comes to what cases we take on. I couldn't have been more clear that working for a witch coven was a bad, a monumentally bad, idea. Yet you grabbed the money at first chance."

"It's a lot of money," Max said. "And no offense, but you don't have to worry about paying bills anymore."

"Bills or not, that doesn't matter. I'm still one of the founders of this agency and I deserve to be heard. Heck, if you didn't have me here, this place would have failed a long time ago."

Sandra sat on the edge of her desk. "I agree. In fact, I think I deserve the same."

Crap. Max hadn't expected to be arguing with both of them at once. "What are you upset at? We took the case."

"I'm not upset. I simply want to point out that I have spent a lot of time studying witchcraft, and I not only contribute to our knowledge of lore but I have on several occasions cast spells that saved us. Like Drummond, this agency would have failed without me."

"Very true," Max said, keeping his voice level. "Both of you are indispensable to our business. I thought you knew that, and I thought we had been good at making sure all our voices were heard."

Drummond swiped off his hat and held it out like a weapon. "The point isn't that I ain't being heard all the time. The point is that you don't listen when it matters. These are witches. You can't trust them."

"Hey, give me a little credit. I know exactly the kind of people we're working for."

"Then why are you doing it?"

Sandra's frown suddenly shifted into open worry. "Hon? Are we having money trouble again?"

The word *again* choked in her throat. Max wanted to rush over, hug her, and assure her that all would be fine. But he remained in his seat. "We're not in a terrible situation. Not yet."

"Not yet?"

"The big chunk of money we got a few years back — we've used up a lot of it. There's still plenty. I mean I'm not worried about us eating tomorrow or anything. But it won't last us more than a few years, and that's provided we don't end up in the hospital or anything serious like that. This isn't news, we've been in this situation for a while."

"How? I thought we had investments, interest, that kind of thing."

"We do. But I'm new to all of that and I made mistakes. I'm still learning."

Picking at his hat, Drummond said, "So you accepted a case from a witch coven because you're worried you'll run out of money in a few years? Sorry, Max, but that's still stupid."

Sandra walked over and kissed the top of his head. "I understand." He knew she did. They had been through enough economic turns together that she had to share the same short-term and long-term fears he held.

"Great," Drummond continued. "You two are all lovey-dovey about taking on a case that might kill you because the money makes you feel secure. I'm so glad we're partners in all of this."

Max shook his head. "Come on, it's not like that. I did hear your concerns and I share them. I haven't been hiding my feelings about witches. Even Sandra's dabbling bothers me."

Sandra's eyes flared. "Don't start that again. That was settled."

"You didn't give me much choice. Basically, I was told you're delving into witchcraft and I better just shut up and like it."

"That's not at all what happened and you know it."

"See?" Drummond shot between them. "This is part of it right here. We haven't even begun working the case and already it's got us at each other's throats. I'm telling you right now, go pick up the phone, call the Mobley Coven and tell them we quit."

The front door burst open and Max's mother rushed in followed by the Sandwich Boys, PB and J. For a fleeting breath, Max thought he had been saved from the argument, but a quick survey of his mother's stern face and the boys' foul moods suggested fighting with Sandra and Drummond would be the lesser pain.

Mrs. Porter stormed over to the coffee maker and slammed through the process of setting it up. "I know I'm the new one around here, but I'm also the oldest among you. You act like I'm fresh off the turnip truck."

PB puffed up his teenage chest. "I don't even know what that means."

Jammer J kept his head low and slunk toward the back corner. He always struck Max as a smart boy, smarter than most, and he continued to prove it by knowing when to get out of the way.

Mrs. Porter turned back with a coffee scoop in her hand. "It means, young man, that I have raised a boy before and I have dealt with stubborn men before and you will not win this. You're going to get registered, and you are going to school."

Max let loose a relieved laugh. "Is that all this is about? You had me thinking something bad had happened."

"Something bad will happen to these boys if nobody starts to take responsibility for them." She curled her lip towards Sandra. "Maybe it's a good thing you two never had kids. You can't even handle boys that are almost grown."

Sandra's entire body went rigid, and Max readied to leap between the two women should it come to actual blows.

"This is stupid," PB said, breaking the tension as he strutted around the room with teenage arrogance. "I been doing just fine without school. Got a job, got a place to live, got enough money to live. Isn't that what school is for? To help you get those kinds of things? Well, I already got them. Seems pretty clear I don't need school's help."

Mrs. Porter gestured to PB like a game show hostess displaying a prize. "Need I say more?"

Sandra's fingers curled into tight fists. In an even tighter voice, she said, "Don't belittle him."

"I'm trying to get through to all of you that these boys need an education. The fact that you can't see that I'm right only further proves the need for a sure hand around here. I'm the only experienced person amongst the lot of you. And if I can raise Max into the fine man he is, I can certainly make the right decisions for these boys. Somebody has to."

Slamming her laptop closed, Sandra gathered up her things. She stomped to the door. "We've got a case that needs some research done. I'll go talk with our clients and get started." She walked out, making sure to give the office door a strong bang.

"Um," Drummond said, "I think I'll take a look around the building. Make sure the office is secure. When you finish in here, I'll be ready to start our end of the investigation."

Max couldn't decide which excuse was more ridiculous, but

he wanted to say something before Drummond left. Talking to a ghost, however, would only upset his mother more. Instead, he got to his feet and approached her. But before he could speak, she put her fists to her hips and leaned forward — a stance he knew too well and it filled him with the same fear he had as a child. He was in trouble.

"Now you listen to me," she began, and he stopped mid-stride. "Your wife is your wife and I'm not going to get in the middle of that. She and I don't agree on much, and that's fine. I can handle the way things are between us all. If your wife wants to be disrespectful to the mother of her husband and you don't wish to defend me, that's fine. Marriage comes with a price and sometimes it's the other members of a family that have to pay it. But these boys should not be the ones to suffer because the two of you can't get your act together."

PB had gravitated toward J. "We don't need school. We're survivors and all school is gonna do is fill us up with nonsense that can't help us out. Not with the kind of lives we got."

"But don't you see?" She brushed by Max and put her arms out to the boys. "An education can change all that. You can have a better life. You can have more."

"Heard it all before. And Jammer J's black. You think he's going to get anything more just because he got an education? Come on." To Max, he added, "You know I'm right. We got a good thing here working for you. Don't let this school thing screw it all up."

Bad enough to be stuck in the middle of this verbal tug-o-war, but Max's mind kept trying to follow Sandra. She could handle talking with the coven just fine, but her entire demeanor struck him as worrisome. They had not talked much about her casting more and more spells, yet he knew she wanted to do so. What if the coven convinced her to become a full-fledged witch?

"Are you even listening to me?" Mrs. Porter said.

"Enough," Max said, startling his mother. "I can't do everything, and right now, I've got to work on a case that's going to pay for all of our food and clothes and such. You boys like being paid regularly, right? Well, this is what I have to do to make sure that happens. So, when it comes to your educations, my mother is in charge." He raised a finger to stop PB's objection. "J is too young to avoid school. PB, you're probably too young also. But there are dropout ages that we can't stop you from leaving school, so we need to find out about that. Don't get your hopes up — I'm pretty sure you've got some school coming your way."

PB's mouth disappeared as his eyes narrowed. "That's not right."

"Maybe, maybe not, but it's the way of it. Mom, you take J with you and get him all squared away. PB will work with me today, and perhaps he and I can talk about this further."

Mrs. Porter clutched J's hand. "I'd rather take care of both boys at the same time. It'll be easier."

"You'll manage."

She paused, perhaps considering whether to argue further, but then she said to J, "Come along."

After they left, PB stormed over to the small bathroom next to the kitchenette. "I'm not going."

"We'll discuss it later. Right now, I've got a secret job for you to do."

PB poked his head out of the bathroom. He couldn't suppress the grin on his face. "I'm in."

Chapter 3

MAX IGNORED PB'S PESTERING as he led the way downstairs to his car parked on the street. He started it up, turned on the air-conditioning, and waited. He could feel PB staring at him, but he said nothing.

After telling PB he had a special mission for the boy, he thought about all that his mother had said. He never liked putting the Sandwich Boys in danger, but he also knew that keeping them on a tight leash would only drive them away. And while he had no misguided view that he was their father, he still felt obligated to be something of a parental figure towards them.

Apparently not enough to put them into school.

The truth there was simple — it never had occurred to him. Why would it? He hadn't spent years raising these boys from infants, learning to care for them, to put their needs before his own, to plan for their futures. He never disciplined them or potty trained them or anything. Really he was just their employer.

Don't start lying to yourself. They're much more than employees.

"Listen," he said, avoiding eye contact. "Before I send you out there on this job, I want you to consider something."

PB screwed his mouth up as he gazed out the side window. "This is about school, isn't it?"

"My mom just wants to look out for you guys. She's not trying to be mean, but sometimes, I guess, as a parent, you have to do the tough things."

"I know that. I'm not mad at her. I don't see the point of school for me, that's all. It's too late."

Max wanted to reach over and hug the boy, but he knew

better. "I don't believe that, but you've got to make your own decisions."

"That's right. I'm practically an adult. Been living like one for years. So let me make up my own mind."

"There's a difference between being an adult and being *practically* an adult, but we can let it rest for now. Any way you cut it, you're not going to school today." Max took a deep breath. "I want you to do something for me, and if you do it right, you'll be fine. But if you screw up, it could be extremely dangerous — to us both."

PB faced Max and put on a serious, firm face. "You can trust me."

"Never doubted it."

"What do I got to do?"

"I want you to follow Sandra. See where she goes, what she's doing, that kind of thing."

PB's eyes widened further than Max thought possible. "You want me to spy on your wife?"

"I know you don't believe in the ghosts and magic and all of that, but you've been around us enough to know that there are people who do believe. They call themselves witches and they practice witchcraft and all of it. Well, those are the types of people we're dealing with on this case. Sandra's really fascinated by them, and that kind of fascination can lead a person to take unwise risks. You follow?"

PB nodded. "You want me to be her backup without her knowing. Protect her, if something goes wrong. That kind of thing."

"Exactly. Watch her and be there to protect her. But mostly just watch her and then report to me. Especially if there's trouble."

"I can handle it."

"I'm sure you can. You'll have to. But don't be foolish enough to take on an entire coven by yourself. You call me for reinforcements. Got it?"

A queasy pallor overcame PB's cheeks. "She's not going to like this."

"That's why it's a secret. You are not to be seen by her. That's the most important part of it."

"I don't know. I want to help, but she's a tough lady. I mean when she's mad — dang, take cover. You know?"

"Of course, I know. But let me make it clearer for you. You have a choice — either go spy on my wife or go to school."

Whipping out his phone, PB said, "What's the coven's address?"

After giving PB the particulars, the boy got out of the car and headed off. Max did not ask how he intended to get all the way to the suburban development. He had learned that he could never stop the boy from certain activities — swiping a car or a bike for a few hours being one of them.

"Have you lost your marbles?" Drummond said appearing in the backseat. "You sent that kid off to spy on Sandra. She's going to kill you both."

"At least then I won't have to worry about my curse."

"Instead, you can worry about me busting your skull every single day for eternity."

"Would you rather I asked you to spy on her?"

"I would've refused."

"Exactly." Max pulled out into traffic and headed south toward the highway — rather than navigate the twists and turns of city streets, it would be faster to jump over to 52 South, get off on Sprague Street, and then pop up to Waughtown. "Do you think I'm wrong? I don't mean the spying — of course, that's wrong — I mean the concern. She's so into the witch side of things, I worry she won't be thinking clear enough to deal with them."

"Hey, I warned you both not to take the case."

"I swear, if you bring that up one more time —"

"Okay, okay." Drummond tapped his pursed lips. "Here's what I really think — you should be worried and you shouldn't be worried."

"Gee, that's a big help."

"Sandra's a tough customer. She might get a bit lost in her head on this one, you're right about that, and I can see why that troubles you. Don't forget, I once dated a witch. It's tricky business. But if there's anybody I ever met that I think could handle the situation, could really dig deep into that world without being seduced by its power, it's Sandra. Heck, she could even be President of the United States and not get corrupted. Maybe. Nah, nobody can handle that job dirt-free."

"I don't care about her being President, I just don't want to lose the woman I love."

Drummond brought his hands together in one firm clap. "You're right. I've been going about this backwards. I shouldn't be berating you for taking the case. I should be helping you solve it. The faster we close this case, the faster we get Sandra away from that coven."

Max drum-rolled his hands on the steering wheel. "Now you're talking."

"Great. Where are we headed?"

"They said Laverne Mobley was going to the pharmacy. So I figured we should check out the pharmacy."

Chapter 4

FROM THE OUTSIDE, the Triad Pharmacy looked like an old bank. All brick with a chimney on the side, the building went with a long and narrow style of architecture. A simple cupola perched atop the roof.

Max exited the car and studied the area. Across Waughtown, he saw a butcher, an auto repair and body shop, and a giant bull statue mounted on two posts. It had brown and white painted fur, horns, and stood even with the telephone lines. The concrete sidewalk stretched up and down the road except for a near-oval section directly in front of the pharmacy. This section had been done with brick, along with the two steps and short wheelchair ramp leading to the entrance.

"Whoever designed this place sure liked brick."

Drummond said, "Your situational awareness sucks. If you paid attention, you'd have seen long ago that most of this town is brick. Reynold's tobacco, Old Salem, schools and warehouses. Bricks everywhere. We probably have more brick homes than any of those northern colonial towns."

"That's really more environmental awareness. Situational awareness is noticing if the guy across the street is acting threatening or not."

"That's odd," Drummond said.

Max thought his partner was setting up another quip, but then he noticed the ghost's inquisitive gaze. "What's wrong?"

"No police. If somebody was kidnapped here, there should be police."

"Maybe it happened elsewhere. On her way here, perhaps."

"No, not on her way. We were told that Laverne called from the pharmacy."

"So then on her way home. Or maybe it did happen here

and the cops have already come and gone. Businesses tend to push the police away as fast as possible — crime scenes aren't good for profits."

Drummond tapped his chin as he floated in front of the building. Max pulled out his phone to take a few pictures — partly because they might need them, mostly because he started getting odd looks from the few pedestrians noticing a man talking to himself on the sidewalk.

"I think we're ignoring the more probable reason," Drummond said in a grim tone that did not match the sunny day surrounding them. "The coven said they didn't want police involvement. So, here we are — no police."

"You think they have a spell to make the police forget about a crime? That's a bit far-fetched."

"Not a spell. Just influence. Mother Hope isn't the only witch out there who tries to control things. And if that's your goal, you've got to have people on the inside of every important government organization — especially, the police."

"Well, if that's the case, if Lena Mobley used her influence to keep the cops away so we can investigate here, then I'm thinking that's what we should do. She's paying the bills on this one."

"Don't remind me."

They entered the building. Icy air prickled Max's skin. At least the owners were not skimping on the air conditioning.

Products of various types lined the walls like a convenience store — from bags of chips to rolls of toilet paper to cans of hairspray. Narrow aisles shelved even more. In the back stood a tall counter separating the main floor from all the actual pharmaceuticals.

Max stepped down an empty aisle and picked up the first item he saw — shaving cream. As he pretended to inspect the label, he muttered, "I don't know what we should do in here. Everything looks normal."

"Keep shopping. I'll recon the building." Drummond slipped off through the walls. Less than a minute later, he returned. "Nothing suspicious in the rest of the building. Not much outside either, but I know what we'll do. It's time for a classic detective technique — lying."

Max smirked. "Tell me what to say."

After a short bit of coaching, Max approached the back counter. A thin gentleman with thinner hair and heavy wrinkles stepped over in a white lab coat. "May I help you?"

Using as much confidence and authority as he could muster, Max said, "I'm Detective Chalmers. A young lady was abducted yesterday morning in this area and I've been asking local businesses to help us create a timeline, perhaps even a pathway that the criminals took."

The man laced his fingers against his stomach. "It's been quiet here."

"I'm sure it has. Otherwise, you would have called us in. But you have surveillance cameras mounted outside." Drummond had spotted the cameras as well as the surveillance recording room set up adjacent to the manager's office in the back. Max continued, "If I could just go over yesterday morning's video, I'll be out of your way as fast as possible."

"I don't know," the man said, looking around for somebody more in charge than himself. "Shouldn't you have a warrant?"

Drummond had anticipated this possibility, so Max followed the ghost's instructions. First, he read the man's nametag — Clarke. Then he said, "Mr. Clarke, I can get a warrant, but that means that I'll have to call a squad car over to sit on this building for the next few hours while I hunt down a judge. We'll have to put up crime scene tape just to be safe — in case a crime did happen here — and it'll remain up until I view the video and determine that everything is fine."

Max had no clue if anything he said would be legal normally, but Mr. Clarke sure believed it. His face dropped. "No, no, that won't be necessary. Please, Detective, come on back."

He escorted Max to the office desk which had a stained computer tower and an ancient, bulky monitor. With several keystrokes and a password, he brought up the video.

"Thank you," Max said.

"I have to be out front for the customers. When you're

done, just leave it on. That computer can be temperamental."

Once Mr. Clarke had left, Max and Drummond settled in front of the screen. Though he shouldn't have expected anything interesting to happen, Max did not prepare for the boredom of watching surveillance footage. Staring at grainy images of the outside walls in real time defined boring.

They knew Laverne had gone to the bank first — she would have used the night deposit slot — and should have arrived at the pharmacy around eight o'clock. They avoided the hours before but then simply had to watch. Minute by minute. Looking for anybody or anything out of the ordinary.

After twenty minutes, Max wondered if they had missed something or they had been wrong about all of it. But a cloaked figure appeared on the screen and Drummond moved in closer. The figure trailed a gloved hand along the wall, ducked under the drive-thru window, and stopped near the top of the screen. When the figure searched around to make sure nobody watched, Max and Drummond got a clear shot of a young lady with an unmistakable, devilish grin — Laverne Mobley.

She bent close to the wall, pressing her face in as if reading tiny print, but her cloak dropped and covered the view. Max squinted out of habit, though doing so did nothing to clean up the image.

"What's she doing?" he asked.

"Don't know. But it can't be anything good."

A black van swept into view, and Drummond pointed at the screen. "This is it."

The side door of the van slid open and two men with ski masks stepped out. Laverne spun around, her hand out like a claw. She said something, and the men hesitated. A bluff. Most spells took too long to cast, but these men did not appear to know it. Or they feared Laverne knew the few fast spells that could hurt them. When a moment passed and they were still fine, they moved in.

One man grabbed her by the arm, yanked her in close, covered her mouth, and wrestled her into the van. At the same time, the other man went to the same section of the wall that she had been inspecting. He crouched down and touched the wall with something metal. The surveillance camera flared bright and when it refocused, the van pulled away leaving nobody behind.

Max paused the video, reset it, and they watched again. "I don't know what to make of that."

Drummond nodded. "We've worked with less."

"True, but that doesn't make it any easier to understand."

Max copied the section of the video onto a thumbdrive. As he left the store, he made sure to thank Mr. Clarke for his assistance. Mr. Clarke seemed only to care that "Detective Chalmers" left quietly and at once.

Outside, Max and Drummond headed around back to the drive-thru windows. They followed the path Laverne had taken, checking the approach, then ducking under the window, and finally stopping where she had been when the van came. Max glanced up and down the paved driveway trying to see if the van had left any marks.

"Look there," Drummond said.

Max knew Drummond stared at the wall, and he also knew he wouldn't like whatever he would see. He turned around. Set low in the wall, enough that one would have to bend over to touch it, Max noted one single brick — blackened and scorched.

"That can't be good."

Chapter 5

MAX PUSHED ASIDE HIS EMPTY PLATE and grabbed a few hushpuppies from the basket. He could feel the little fingers of deep fried cornmeal hardening his arteries, but hushpuppies were among the many wonders of Southern cuisine that he could not deny. Plus, having such a late lunch opened him to eating too fast and too much.

"You finished your burger, so can we get started?" Drummond had endured sitting amongst all the food passing their booth. Diner food, in particular, struck a hard string in the old ghost — too much like the world he lived in long ago.

Wiping his mouth, Max opened his laptop and loaded the video from the thumbdrive. Drummond eased straight through the table so that he could see the screen. Together, they watched as Laverne skirted along the wall, ducked under the window, and stopped at the brick. Her cloak fell to block her activities. The van arrived, the men went into action, the flash of light, and they were gone.

"Play it again," Drummond said.

Seeing where this would lead, Max set the viewer on a continuous loop. Over and over the abduction played out. Each time, Max tried to focus on a different aspect of the crime. He looked for a license plate — it didn't show clear enough in the footage. He looked for the driver — the man never got out of the van. He looked for shadows of other people who might have witnessed the incident — nobody.

As Laverne started her approach to the brick once more, Max popped another hushpuppy in his mouth. "Maybe this is a straightforward kidnapping. Maybe these idiots had no clue Laverne was a witch."

"You may want to keep those thoughts a bit quieter around

here."

Max choked on his food. Glancing around, he saw a few diners staring at him but otherwise, nobody cared. Stupid — he had been so wrapped up in the video, he forgot that he sat in a public place.

In a lower voice, he said, "What about it, though? You think they picked the wrong hostage?"

"No." Drummond watched closely as the van pulled into view. "They knew enough to do something to that brick, so they knew she was a witch. Maybe knew she was part of the Mobley Coven, too."

"What about that brick, anyway? You ever see anything like that?"

He shook his head. "I thought it might be a Call to Power thing like we saw with those bones of the Alamance soldiers but that required a whole ritual and spell to work."

"It also used blood, and that time, the magic infused in those bones caused the bones to break apart when they released. This brick didn't shatter or anything."

"Yeah. It looked more like it had been cooked." Once more, Laverne ducked under the window and approached the special brick. "Maybe we have it backwards. Maybe she was casting a spell onto the brick and got interrupted."

"Possible. Then the van shows up, they take her, and they do something to ruin her spell which causes a flash and burn reaction. I can buy that."

"Either way, we don't really know. We should show this to Sandra as soon as possible. There might be enough here for her to figure it out."

"That reminds me," Max said and pulled out his cellphone. "I need to check in with PB."

Though Drummond said nothing, Max could feel the ghost's disapproval. Well, he was dead. He didn't have to worry about all the mundane parts of a life. He didn't have to consider how empty it would all feel without Sandra. Heck, if Max and Sandra died, Drummond would get to spend eternity with them.

As he punched in PB's number, his chest lumped with guilt. He knew better than to think so ill of Drummond. It wasn't the ghost's fault that Sandra's interest in witchcraft bothered Max so much or that Max's worry led to behavior that he knew to be wrong. If anything, Drummond had tried to look out for him.

"Hey, Bossman," PB said.

Watching Drummond watch the video, Max said, "You got anything to report?"

"She's been going around town talking to a bunch of women, one after the other. Some were really old bats, kind of weird looking. I'm guessing they all think they're witches. I mean the one lady only had one eye and she was all hunched over. Another waved a wooden cane around like she could shoot magic out of it or something. It's crazy."

"I know it seems that way, but thanks for putting up with it. You're doing a good job — keep on it. If I don't call you by the time it gets dark and Sandra's still talking to these women, give me a call."

"You got it, Bossman."

As Max ended the call, he snickered. PB would work extra hard for him the next few weeks. Anything to show Max that he didn't need to go to school.

But Max's mother had a point. Even if it turned out that PB could legally drop out, Max wondered if he should intervene. After all, he and Sandra were the only things resembling parents to these boys. Perhaps they should start acting like it.

"There," Drummond said. In his excitement to freeze the video, he smacked the keyboard causing a jolt of pain through his ghostly form — ghosts and the corporeal world did not like to come into actual contact. Sucking on his fingers, he motioned for Max to stop the video and reverse for a bit. After a moment, he pointed straight at the screen.

"What is it?" Max said. He saw the van with the door open and the man holding Laverne from behind — same as the other hundred times he had watched the video.

"Look at his forearm, the one across Laverne's shoulders."

Despite the rough quality of the image, Max saw the distinct shades of a tattoo. "Can you make out what it is? If we know that we can try to search for the artist who made it. Not easy, but not impossible. Worst situation, we have to call every tattoo parlor in North Carolina."

"No need. I know exactly what I'm looking at and exactly where we need to go next."

"You going to share this information?"

Drummond cocked an eyebrow. "That's a tattoo of a flaming cross. Belongs to only one group I've ever heard of, and they took Laverne to their only real gathering spot. It's a series of rundown warehouses in Lexington."

"Great. And who are they?"

"They're witch hunters."

Chapter 6

MAX DROVE SOUTH ON 85 until he reached the exit for Lexington. Following Main Street into the city, he then shifted over a block, across railroad tracks, and onto Elk Street. From there, it took only a minute before he pulled up to an old tobacco warehouse. Standing tall and cavernous, the brick building had long, narrow windows — most of which had been shattered by vandals. The railroad poked out of the grass and ran by the back of the building. Faded paint on one outside wall boasted *Kapl Tobac - supplier for Reynold's Tob.*

"This is the place," Drummond said as he appeared in the passenger seat. "Kaplan Tobacco. They were a private farming operation that Reynolds used a while back. Kaplan was one of the key men responsible for forming the Goodman Witch Hunters. I swear I thought I'd never have to deal with them again."

Max went to the trunk of the car to prepare. He had a few bags packed with the items they regularly needed including a flashlight, a shovel, and a .38 — in addition to training at martial arts, he and Sandra had agreed to start learning to shoot. Not that ghosts could be harmed by bullets, but they had encountered many living beings that had no problem firing off rounds in their direction. They both thought being able to fire back with some degree of competence made sense.

But he had to admit that he lacked skill with his ability to handle a gun. Still, he holstered the weapon — he could use it to threaten somebody, at the least. He picked up a shoulder bag that had a first aid kit and some water inside. If things went well and Max retrieved Laverne, she might need those items. Last, he grabbed the flashlight.

As he strode across the weeds toward the building,

Drummond said, "Back in my day, these guys were not to be trifled with. One of them somehow fell into knowing about witches and he convinced the others he was telling the truth. Not too hard, really. People tend to scare easy — especially when their prosperity is at stake."

Max pulled open a rotting, wooden door. Though the sun came through the window openings, Max clicked on his flashlight. He entered a dust-covered office room. Another door on the opposite side led to the warehouse.

"At first," Drummond went on, "these guys were mostly a nuisance and nothing more. They'd try to get information, try to find a witch, that kind of thing, but back in those days, the Hull family controlled all the magic dealing in the city. They made sure to divert these men from stumbling too far into a fateful mess."

Max opened the door slowly. The warehouse looked empty and unused. Dust covered most of the floor. Huge racks rose toward the ceiling used for drying out tobacco leaves. Keeping his flashlight low to the floor, Max moved toward the end of one rack.

Drummond said, "But these boys were worse than a dog with a meaty bone. It turned into a weekly event for them. Every Saturday night they'd go to the bar, get drunk, and go witch hunting. Of course, the witches knew to be watching for these fellas, so the guys never caught anybody."

Peeking down one long rack, Max thought he caught a glimpse of movement.

"Well, I knew trouble would be coming along eventually. I tried to talk some sense into them, but it went nowhere. Probably the whole thing would've petered out but one day they actually managed to stumble upon a witch in the woods. She was in the middle of casting a spell and they were fall-down drunk. Nobody really knows if she cast a spell at them or if they just panicked and ran, but one of the guys — Bobby Goodman — never made it out. They found him with his neck snapped."

Max paused to look at Drummond. "He tripped, didn't he?

Tripped and broke his own neck."

"That's my guess, but they didn't take it like that. Finally named themselves the Goodman Witch Hunters and they went out strong the next several nights. They eventually caught a young lady, took her here, to their hideout-clubhouse thing. Tied her to a stake and burned her alive. But it turned out, she wasn't a witch. Just a gal in the wrong place at the wrong time."

Max glanced back down the rack. Again, he saw that movement. Somebody was definitely at the other end of the warehouse.

"After that death and the investigation, it took little to break a confession from one of them. They all ended up doing time. That ended Kaplan Tobacco and it ended the Goodman Witch Hunters. At least, I thought so. Clearly, they raised another generation or two to keep up the fight."

In a soft whisper, Max said, "Will you please go down to the other end and tell me what's there? I keep seeing something move."

Drummond slid back a few inches. "That's not a good idea. Not for me. If these are descendants of the original witch hunters, they've had a long time to branch out into other paranormal interests — like ghosts. I don't want know what ways they may have learned to hurt my kind."

Clenching his jaw, Max said, "Fine. We'll do it the old fashioned way."

He pulled out the .38 and started toward the back of the warehouse. Several feet closer. He could hear his own breathing grow harder. The cool air of Drummond following from behind only doubled his nerves — anything that scared Drummond frightened Max.

A clang echoed through the building. Max froze in place. Somebody had dropped a metal object — loud enough to be a crowbar or even a heavy-duty, long-necked flashlight.

"Either turn back or keep going," Drummond said. "Standing still ain't a good choice."

Max licked his lips and walked forward. About halfway across, he reached the end of the one rack. There was a wide space cutting across and then another rack started. From what he could tell, the person making the noise stood at the end of the next rack, one aisle over.

Max shut off his flashlight — he had enough sunlight to guide him and too many nerves to keep the beam steady anyway. He let out a long breath but his hand still shivered. The .38 grew heavier with each second. He had been shot at before, he had held a gun before, but rarely had the two coincided.

He wanted to turn away and leave. He could observe the warehouse from a safe distance, watch who left the building, and then inspect the empty warehouse at his leisure. But that meant letting this man escape and probably meant allowing greater harm to come to Laverne.

"You can do this," Drummond said — no judgment in his tone. "You've faced down a lot worse than a thug with a gun."

Max nodded, swallowed down the lump in his throat, and jumped into the aisle. Brandishing his .38, he said, "Freeze!"

The single word reverberated throughout the warehouse. All his fear and anguish and adrenaline echoed off the walls, repeating those emotions back upon him. Before him, a shadowed figure with hands raised slowly turned.

"Max?"

Sandra? Max's heart skipped and he fumbled the .38. It hit the floor and shot off to the side. He yipped in surprise and Sandra jumped at the gunblast.

Seven minutes followed as the two hugged and calmed their frayed nerves. They laughed out their anxiety and sighed out their fears.

"You two are lucky that gun didn't kill one of you," Drummond said, but Max detected some extra relief in the ghost's voice as well.

After they had regained their composure, Sandra led Max and Drummond further along the aisle. "We're too late," she said.

Laverne Mobley's body lay on the cold floor as if she had fallen from a great height. Her legs and arms had been broken, and her eyes remained open wide. Water soaked her clothes and hair. Strangest of all, however, was her skin.

Sunken cheeks and eyes. Dark purple bruising and pale white flesh pressed tight to the bones. Her emaciated form looked fragile and incomplete. Her wet clothing clung against her with large folds — too big for her shrunken body. Rope burns marred her wrists and ankles. The stench of Death emanated from her as if she had suffered from a plague for years before finally succumbing.

Max covered his nose and mouth. "Looks like these witch hunters are playing with some witchcraft of their own."

Drummond floated over the corpse. "It's certainly not a natural death. But I find it hard to believe that a Goodman hunter could have done this. That would go against everything they stand for."

"No offense, but a group created by a bunch of drunken idiots looking to pass the time by hurting people is not really the kind of thing that has a strong moral center. They don't stand for anything but getting an excuse for violence."

Looking up from her phone, Sandra said, "I got a text from Lena."

"Wait a minute," Max said, happy for any reason to step away from the horrid sight of Laverne's body. "What were you doing here? I mean how did you even know to get here?"

"I did my research, same as you."

"Yeah, but we only found out because of the surveillance video and an arm tattoo. What clued you into coming here? It might help us —"

"We can talk about that later. We've got a big problem." She tapped out a reply to Lena.

Drummond swished behind her. "What is it, doll?"

"Looks like another witch has gone missing."

Chapter 7

MAX AND SANDRA EACH DROVE THEIR CARS out to a rundown strip mall in Archdale — a town near High Point about twenty minutes north of Lexington. The place had a few stores clinging to life but the torn up parking lot, the smashed signage, and sorry state of the blue roof all pointed to an owner who no longer cared what happened to the property. It also made for an excellent meeting spot. At least, that was the explanation Lena offered for choosing the location.

Max didn't care where they met. He wanted some answers.

The strip mall sat at the bottom of an incline with the main road running by at the top. Across the street and on either side, burger joints, gas stations, and all manner of businesses thrived. Only this lone strip mall suffered. The idea that this section of land might have been cursed, perhaps even by the Mobley Coven, crossed Max's mind. As Lena drove down in her minivan, looking more like a suburban mom than before, he struggled to make the two versions of her blend. Regardless, witch or cliché, he kept in mind she was dangerous.

However, as she stepped from the car, the quiver in her chin and the way her eyes darted around undercut any bravado she may have held. "Please tell me you've found them," she said, her voice catching at the end. "Tell me something."

Max set his laptop on the hood of his car. "You seem a lot more upset than you were this morning."

"I'm the house sister of the coven. I have to keep things in order, keep things running."

Sandra put a hand on Lena's shoulder. "You have to keep everybody calm, don't you?"

"If they knew how terrified I am of what's happening, if they knew how much I feared we might be seeing the beginning of something horrible — well, I don't want to be blamed for causing panic in the coven. So, please, tell me what you found."

"Don't buy it," Drummond said. "If a witch is telling you how scared she is, then you should be the one shaking."

Max brought up the surveillance video. "This is Laverne from this morning. I need you to watch it and tell me everything you see."

The video played out, and Lena gasped as the men jumped out of the van. When the one man lowered in front of the brick and the camera flared, Lena's entire body froze. She lost all her nervous energy and turned cold.

"I see," she said.

"We don't. Maybe you can help us. Do you know who these men are? Do you know what the deal is with that brick?"

"I'm sorry. I don't."

Drummond clicked his tongue. "I hope I don't have to point out that she's lying."

"Please," Sandra said, "any details will help."

Max paused the video to display the man's tattoo. "Have you ever seen that mark before?"

"Never," Lena said.

"I think you have seen it. I think you know that it belongs to the Goodman Witch Hunters, and I also think you know what that means for Laverne."

Lena's focus snapped toward Max, her mouth wide open. "She's dead, isn't she?"

"Something drained her life away and left behind a broken shell. It wasn't a normal death. What did they do to her? What kind of spell could cause that?" Lena stepped away, but Max followed. "You hired us, spent a lot of money on us, so that we could help you. But we can't do anything if you're going to withhold key information. Laverne died today because we wasted time finding out about the Goodman hunters. You could have told us —"

"I didn't know." She looked to Sandra. "Where is Laverne now? I'll send my people to collect her before the police get involved."

Sandra wrote down the address and handed it over with a gentle nod. "Warn them to be very careful. These witch hunters might be waiting."

"Don't worry about that. We can handle ourselves when we know what to expect."

Max snatched the laptop and tossed it in his car. "I guess we're all done. If you won't give us all the information we need to work this case, there's no point in continuing."

"Amen to that," Drummond said.

Lena's lip curled as if she had wanted Max to threaten leaving. "Mr. Porter, you must understand that a coven exists in secrecy for very good reasons. We have a long, dark history of being mistreated by outsiders."

Max thought of the door warded against ghosts in the coven's house. "I would think my wife's presence and knowledge would ease your concerns."

"They do. But a coven must keep its secrets. Now, if Sandra were to join our coven, then all we know would be bared open to her. And, sadly, Laverne's death creates an opening spot in our ranks."

Expecting Sandra to politely decline, Max stayed quiet. But the silence grew. Sandra said nothing.

The world slowed as he turned towards her. She seemed to be weighing the offer — actually weighing it in her head as if there were some possibility that he would accept her doing such a thing. Lena put out her hand and Sandra licked her lips. Max wanted to scream out, lunge forward, and break through whatever spell his wife had fallen under.

A spell? Unless he was the one falling prey. The voice of his wife sounded tiny and far away. He tried to move his arms but they held still.

"Thank you," Sandra said, "but I'm not the coven type."

Like a popping balloon, Max heard a loud snap and everything returned to normal — the sounds, the pace, everything moved as it should. He studied his team — nobody had noticed anything. But the smirk on Lena's face suggested she knew. Of course, she did. She had to have been the one casting the spell. But could she do it when there was no casting circle, no uttered words, no sign of any kind to indicate a spell? Or perhaps one of her coven sisters hid nearby, casting the spell on her behalf.

With a frustrated pout, Lena said, "I'm sorry to hear that. The offer will remain open as long as we have the spot to fill."

"Great," Drummond said. "She can put up a recruitment poster. Let's leave."

But Sandra stepped closer to Lena. "You still have a missing witch. We understand — I understand the need for secrecy, but you're going to have to decide what is more important to the coven — secrecy or protecting one of your own."

Rolling her mouth while offering an erudite nod, Lena said, "They are often the same thing."

"Not in this case."

"Especially in this case. But I suppose I do need to give you some information. As your husband pointed out, you can't be expected to do your job without at least some relevant facts."

Drummond circled from above. "No, no, no. We're done here. They paid for us to find Laverne and we did."

Lena said, "The woman's name is Candace Mobley. She is a short, rotund woman. Light-skinned black. Sweet and lovely woman and a very capable witch."

"When and where was she last seen?" Sandra asked.

"She left a little before Laverne."

"It's obvious somebody is targeting your coven. You need to get the word out to the rest of your sisters and make sure everyone is on alert."

"Yes, of course. And remember that we do not want the police involved at all."

"You have my word."

Lena turned to her car and chuckled. "Be careful yourself. You should never give anything freely to a witch — even your word."

After she drove away, Drummond swooped down in front of Sandra. "Why did you do that? We could have been done with this and you went ahead — again, without consulting anybody else — and decided to keep us stuck working for a witch coven."

Sandra put a hand on her hip — a clear sign of her anger. "Just because these women are witches doesn't mean they don't deserve help."

"Doll, that's exactly what it means. They made a choice to delve into the darker worlds and that brings a cost. It's dangerous."

"We do it all the time."

"For different reasons. We're not trying to gain power over anybody or manipulate the natural balance of life. When we're forced to use magic or deal with those darker worlds, we do so in order to protect people, to right wrongs, and all that noble kind of thing."

With the fuzzy, odd sensations leaving his head, Max said, "No use in arguing about it. Sandra gave her word and I'm pretty sure we can't go back on that now. Not without repercussions. So, let's work this second case, hope we do better, and then I'm with Drummond — after the case, we need to be done with this coven."

Crossing his arms, Drummond looked off into the distance. "Fine. So long as your wife accepts that last part."

Before Sandra could launch into an angry tirade, Max jumped in. "We don't have much to go on in finding Candace. Seems like our best bet is with the Goodman hunters. But other than an abandoned warehouse, what do we know?"

"They drive a van," Drummond said.

Though still upset, Sandra faced Max to do her job. "We also know that the Goodman hunters have some ability with magic — unless they carried an arc-welder with them to burn out that brick."

Max tapped his chin with his knuckles. "I see three things for us to do. Drummond, can you look into these new Goodmans. See what you can find about who they are and if they have another place like the warehouse. I'm going to research the Mobley Coven. Seems to me that if somebody is after them, we should know more about what they've been doing and what they've done. It might lead us to answers. And Sandra, maybe you can do some of your real estate voodoo and figure out who owns that warehouse now. See if they're connected to the Goodman hunters."

"I've got it. I know who to talk to."

"Going to interview more witches?"

Both of Sandra's hands went to her hips. "I knew it! Twice today I swore I saw PB in the distance, but then I thought that no way would my husband be such a stupid twit as to have PB spy on me."

Drummond shook his head at Max. "You should listen to me more often."

"You knew?" Sandra snapped towards the ghost. "And you let him to do this?"

"He's a grown boy. He can make his own stupid decisions."

"You should've stopped him."

Max reached out towards her. "Honey, it's not like that. I was worried about you. This isn't like the dabbling in witchcraft from before. This is hardcore stuff. I mean it's not even as simple as a run-of-the-mill witch coven. If what we were told is true, the Mobley Coven is one of the most serious out there. Of course, I worried about you."

She let his hands hang alone in the air. "That sounds nice and respectable, but it isn't. Despite all I've done for this group, you still act like I can't handle myself."

"I know. I'm sorry. What can I do?"

"Stop acting like a jerk, for once. Go do your research and allow me to do mine. And if I ever catch you sending spies on me again, you'll have a lot worse to fear than all the horrible things we've seen over the years."

Whirling away, she fumed off to her car. "Don't wait up."

Max stood in the cratered parking lot as Sandra screeched her wheels before speeding away. He did not move for a bit, his head feeling as assaulted as when Lena had cast her spell.

Floating up next to him, Drummond sighed. "I told you so."

Chapter 8

THE DRIVE HOME DID NOTHING TO CALM MAX. Everything about the current situation bothered him — working for a coven, the strange way Laverne Mobley had died, the spell or attempted spell cast upon him, and most of all, Sandra. She had every right to be mad at him, and yet, part of him thought she should be more understanding. It wasn't as if he had sent a PI because he feared she might be cheating on him. He sent PB to make sure she didn't get hurt by witches.

But perhaps that wasn't the complete truth.

He feared what he had seen in her eyes when Lena offered a spot in the coven — desire. That emotion could draw one into deep waters, catch one in a strong undertow, drown one in murky depths. He had sent PB to watch over her, see that she did not lose herself. Make sure she remained Max's loving wife.

Drummond had been kind enough, or smart enough, to stay away for the drive home. Hopefully, the ghost went about his task and was looking into the Goodman Witch Hunters. But even if he simply went into the Other to hang out with the rest of the ghostly dead, Max appreciated the quiet.

After parking the car, he entered the house and discovered his mother and the Sandwich Boys cleaning dishes in the kitchen. "Why are you eating here?" he blurted out.

Mrs. Porter jumped and sudsy water puffed from the sink. "Don't go scaring an old lady like that. You'll send me to the hospital."

"Sorry. I only meant that, well, you've got an apartment now. The boys have their own place. Why are you all hanging out here?"

"Well, we had hoped to surprise you with some dinner, but nobody came home and we got hungry. Isn't that right, boys?

Of course, if you had bothered to call, we could have cleared the whole thing up, but that's the way of things. You wouldn't be the first parent to disappoint his kids by failing to show up to a celebration."

"I'm not a parent," Max said, setting his laptop on the kitchen counter. Rubbing the side of his head and wanting to simply be alone, he forced a smile. "What are we celebrating?"

Jammer J set plates into the dishwasher. "I'm going to school tomorrow!"

"That's great." He knew he sounded beat, but he tried to pay attention.

"We got me all registered and they had this kid, Chris, who showed me around the school. It's really big. They got baseball fields and soccer fields and a computer lab and a big cafeteria and every kid gets their own locker. Oh, and I got my classes, too."

PB punched J in the arm. "You're such a nerd. Who cares about classes?"

"You will," Mrs. Porter said. "Tomorrow I'm taking you in to register and get you started, too."

"But I'm working for Max. You can't take me off a case. I'll worry about school next week."

"Look at J. He's your best friend, and he's thrilled to know he's going to learn new things and meet other children his own age."

PB forced a smile. "That's him. Not me."

"We've talked about this. You need —"

"I'm not doing it." He jutted his chin out.

"You most certainly will. I won't be a party to watching you fail to live up to your potential. Max, tell this young man what's what. I raised you and I know what I'm talking about. PB, you've got a sharp mind. School will make it like a sword."

"Bossman, c'mon," PB said, getting right up into Max's face. "You know you need me. I've helped on a ton of cases. You really going to let me be carted off to some school where they'll warp my brain into being another corporate cog?"

Pushing aside his shock at how tall PB had become, Max

forced his words out through gritted teeth. "You're talking about junior high and high school. They're so far from corporate cogs, it's laughable."

"You're laughing at me now?"

"If you think so, then you really do need to go school."

Mrs. Porter dried her hands on a dish towel. "I really don't see why you are making such a fuss. Young J is going to surpass you if you don't go. And look how excited and happy he is."

"Bossman, I'm telling you this is a mistake. You need me."

"Do I?" Max snapped. "Because if you'd bother to look around, you'd notice that my wife is not here. You know why? Do you?"

PB inched away. "Is everything okay?"

"No. It's not. You were supposed to be a shadow. Instead you might as well have flashed the sun in her eyes. She saw you. And now she's pissed off at me. So, don't go telling me how indispensable you are. In fact, if you really have any sense about you, you'd realize that my mother is right. You need to go to school. Maybe then you'll learn how to do your job."

The instant the words were out, Max wished he could reel them back. He could read PB's hurt too well and it broke his heart. He might as well have slapped the boy across the face.

PB lowered his head, ashamed and fearful. Of course, he was afraid. If Max fired him, he would have no income, no way to pay for the ratty place he lived in; he would end up back on the streets.

"Come on, boys," Mrs. Porter said, gathering their things together. "It's obvious Max has had a long, hard day and is saying things he doesn't mean. Besides, you two need to get a good night's sleep, so you'll be refreshed and ready to take on tomorrow. It'll be a big day for you both."

Jammer J hurried out and Mrs. Porter followed. She stopped at the front door. "PB? Come on, now."

PB glared at Max, but he couldn't sustain the anger. His eyes glistened and he rushed off before a tear could drop down his cheek.

"Shit," Max said to the empty kitchen.

For a full two minutes, he stood motionless, trying to understand how suddenly he felt the guilt of a father who had screwed up with his teenage son. It made sense that they had become protective of the boys, perhaps even in a parental way, and he had no doubts that they all considered each other family. But he never tried to be their father. Good or bad, those boys had fathers, and it wasn't Max's place to take the job over. He could be a mentor, a boss, a friend, and more, but not a father.

From the back of one of the top cabinets, Max pulled out a bottle of Noah's Mill bourbon — smooth with hints of rye and vanilla. He poured two fingers and gulped it down. After coughing for a moment — he forgot that his secret bourbon rated 114 proof — he took a breath and shook his head clear. As the burn in his stomach spread into warmth throughout, he grabbed the laptop and entered his study.

Regardless of how poorly Max had handled the situation, the fact remained that PB needed to go to school. It was that simple. It had to be because Max needed to push that problem aside so he could refocus on his wife and the Mobley Coven.

He slapped the laptop onto his desk and yanked the top open. Those witches had taken too much of an interest in Sandra. No way would he let some coven take his wife away. She always said he had one superpower, and he intended to use it.

Max Porter sat at his desk and started to research the Mobley Coven.

Chapter 9

BY MIDNIGHT, Max had to look away from the screen. His eyes had dried out, his neck ached, and his lower back threatened to seize up if he didn't stretch. Rolling his head in a circle and rubbing his shoulders, he walked into the kitchen.

Hours of searching the internet, of rethinking search terms, of reworking search parameters, of thinking he had finally found them only to discover a dead end — it all left his head throbbing. He poured a glass of water and nursed it by the sink.

Any witch coven that had managed to survive more than a generation would be difficult to find information about — actual witch hunts tended to make covens secretive. Since the Mobley Coven's reputation suggested they had been around for several generations, they had to be even better at keeping a low profile. If they hadn't hired the Porter Agency, Max would never have heard the name Mobley or known their address.

But I do have the name Mobley and the address of their current residence.

The name. Max hurried back to his desk. All the sisters carried the same surname — Mobley. Of course, they were not all actual sisters, rather they were sisters of the same coven. Since this sorority of spellwork behaved like a tight-knit family, Max thought it likely that some of them — the most devout — might legally have changed their last name to Mobley in a fit of loyalty.

After only a few keystrokes, he found fifty legal registrations of the name change in North Carolina over the course of several decades. With previous names in hand, Max traced back their lives through census information, birth announcements, obituaries, news reports, and numerous other sources he often used. Because the women involved in the coven never married, or if they did, they never took on a husband's surname, the paths went back quite far with many less detours than he usually encountered.

Around two in the morning, Max had reached the end of the trail — Eunice Mobley. Born to Abraham and Elmira Mobley in 1877. They lived and worked a small farm set between Winston-Salem and Kernersville.

"Now I've got you," Max said.

He closed all the programs on his desktop and clicked on the Tor Browser. This browser utilized other computers in order to bounce and hide its identity. While not entirely anonymous, the Tor browser was a favorite among criminals, conspiracy theorists, and anybody who wanted to hide their activities from over-reaching governments. Also a regular user — witches. This was an entryway into the darknet, and if Max had any hope of finding details about the Mobley Coven it would be on the darknet.

Much of the darknet could not be searched. A known web address was the only reliable way to find information. But when it came to the world of witches, several search sites had been developed for their private use. Hence, the darknet.

Max had learned about this site from Sandra. Trying to ignore how that fact burrowed into his chest, he brought up the website and first searched for a Mobley Coven website. Several covens ran their own websites on the regular internet, but they tended to be more hobbyists or religious Wiccan than actual, spellcasting witches. Like much of the witchcraft information online, these sites leaned toward the practical, herbal, and New Age-types of things. A few sites Sandra regularly used had access to ancient texts and such but you had to know what you were doing to make real use of them.

On the darknet, however, the other kind of covens resided. To an extent. Not surprisingly, most covens kept off the internet and darknet when it came to internal matters. The real source of their history, spellwork, membership, and all other valuable information would be written on paper and bound in their grimoire — a coven's book of family secrets. But that didn't stop the researchers of the world from compiling whatever information they could get a hold of, and that was where Max struck gold.

On a darknet site called The Unrecorded History, several university professors from various disciplines traded research that they could not publish in journals without destroying their reputations and probably losing their jobs. But through one experience or another, they had come to know the reality of witches, spells, ghosts, and more. They needed answers and so they turned to each other for help.

Max clicked on a link appropriately titled Covens and found an alphabetical listing of over two thousand documented witch covens. Scrolling down, he found the entry *Mobley Coven*, clicked on it, and marveled at the first picture he ever saw of Eunice Mobley.

She stood in front of a barn with three other women — all appeared to be in their twenties. The caption read: Eunice Mobley (center) with three unidentified women. Thought to be near Greensboro, though not the Mobley family farm which was sold years earlier. Possibly near turn of century.

For the very late-1800s, Eunice looked scandalous. Her dress, make-up, and hair would have been more appropriate decades later during the Roaring 20s. The defiance in her eyes suggested she knew and didn't care that people might see this photograph. But at the same time, the other women looked like they were having fun being naughty, that they knew this was a little secret dress-up and photo, and that the moment they finished, several of them would wish the photograph didn't exist.

"So, even at the beginning, you could get some women to bend to your will," Max said to the screen.

Reading through the history of the coven, he took notes so that he would remember what to share with Sandra and Drummond later. It whirled in his head like a gathering storm. He wrote furiously to keep from losing his momentum, part of him fearing that should he stop, should he close his eyes even for a few minutes, when he woke, he would find the website gone, spelled away into a darker net that could never be found.

It began with Eunice Mobley.

According to the scholarly research, Eunice showed a rebellious attitude from early on. She often would be found at the center of trouble yet blame rarely fell upon her shoulders. This tendency culminated in the drowning of Elizabeth Miner. While the death had been ruled accidental, journals and diaries of locals suggested otherwise. Many people thought that Eunice had been responsible. They thought it often enough and strongly enough that they wrote it down. The two girls were rivals for the affections of Johnathan Short, and as one diary put it: *That girl has the Devil inside her. She'd kill her own kin if it meant getting a new dress or some other trinket she wanted. So there is no misbegotten thought of mine that she had some hand in poor Lizzie's passing. I can only pray that the good Lord will see justice done where none can be found elsewhere.*

Eunice must have figured out that the town had reached their boiling point with her. She left the Kernersville area and moved to the far end of Greensboro. While one town over did not really constitute "getting out of Dodge," back then, even a short distance could feel far.

Much of her life disappeared from any record the historians could find with the exception of one photograph. It depicted her standing arm-in-arm with a short, unidentified woman. They both wore white nightgowns and stood in front of a window. Max studied the photo, attempting to pick out details of what lay on the other side of the window, but he could only see blurs.

The short woman also took his interest. She reminded him of one of the ladies in the previous photograph, but everything in this woman's countenance held more strength, more power, more zest for life. Particularly, her eyes. They defined the term *piercing* and seemed to cut through his computer screen to prick his skin and draw a bead of blood. Not a woman he ever wanted to face. If she were alive, she'd be well over a hundred, and Max suspected she could still strike fear with those eyes.

When the trail of Eunice's history re-emerged, she had a

new interest in the occult — specifically witchcraft. Any books she could acquire, any person she could talk with, she sought them out. Over the next two decades, her interest turned into obsession and eventually, she stopped learning about the subject and began practicing it. Though much of those details were inferred from diaries and newspaper articles, Max agreed with the conclusions. It helped that he knew this woman's legacy ended up with a coven still in existence bearing her name.

During Eunice's early dabbling in witchcraft, however, nobody knew how she supported herself. She did not marry nor was their evidence of her prostituting herself. She held no employment, either.

"I know what you did," Max said.

Considering where her life would lead, he thought she surely sold spells, potions, charms, and curses. Perhaps even accepted money to do some palm reading and other entertainment-type prognostication. It would have been done in secret. Between the Moravians, the Quakers, and the Hull family, any hint of witchcraft would have been met with harsh consequences.

That seemed the likely explanation for her next move. She left the southeastern edge of Greensboro for a cabin in the wooded northern section. Max pictured the spooky walk through the woods that the desperate would make until they found the solitary cabin. They would knock on the splintered door with a shaking hand, and when they entered, they would have no idea they had entered a spider's web that would never let them free. Bargaining with a witch always brought pain.

Perhaps that existence went on for years. Somewhere along the line, however, Eunice grew weary of her position in the world. She wanted more. Of everything.

While the exact date of the founding of Mobley Coven was unknown, the historians pinpointed it between the late-1910s and early-1920s. From the start, she insisted that all her sisters take her name. That helped narrow the years, but the biggest clue came from the reaction of people.

It was one thing to be a scary witch living off in the

wilderness. It was another to have a coven, a private army of witches willing to follow commands with the blind loyalty of a cult. But by the mid-1920s, the Mobley Coven disappeared from Greensboro after an unexplained fire consumed the cabin and fears surrounding them also died out.

Until they next popped up in Winston-Salem in the 1940s. Presumably, the coven had continued to operate throughout the intervening decades, but it wasn't until World War II that the witches began to ply their trade again in a noticeable way. Spells, charms, curses, fortune telling — there were plenty of frightened soldiers wanting supernatural insurance before they headed off to war. After D-Day, there were even more wives and girlfriends wanting the same.

This pattern repeated itself over and over. The coven would disappear from notice, still working but keeping to the shadows, until a major event — Korea, Cuba, Vietnam, 9-11, Iraq, Afghanistan — brought them out in full force. As one of the most powerful covens in the South, it did not surprise Max that they were in high demand.

One thing — one thing of many — troubled him. Why did the Hulls allow the Mobley Coven to exist? Until recent events involving the Porter Agency, the Hull family had controlled all magic in North Carolina. No witches practiced without the Hulls knowing about it and consenting to it. What benefit could they derive from permitting a coven to become powerful?

"Unless they didn't know." Max leaned his chair back, his fingers laced behind his head, and looked off in thought. Could the Mobley Coven have somehow kept their existence secret even from the Hulls?

The clatter of the front door locks snapped Max out of his musing. He checked the clock — 4:21 am. Sandra finally had come home.

He wanted to call her over to the study, show her what he had found, and most of all, ask her about the possibilities. She would know if a coven could simultaneously be well-known enough to have soldiers and lovers calling on them yet keep the prying eyes of the Hulls away.

Except Sandra's tired footsteps clumped upstairs. Coupled with their recent argument, she would be too exhausted to listen without the conversation turning ugly. Max kept quiet.

Instead, he returned to his laptop, ready to shut it down and get some sleep. Probably on the couch. Yet he saw a late entry from a professor in California. She had taken all the known information about the cabin where the Mobley Coven had been founded and tried to locate where it might have been. She detailed her methods, and in the end of several long and technical paragraphs that left Max dizzy, she pinpointed a spot at 36° 07'50"N 79° 50'03.1"W.

Max copied the coordinates, shut down the darknet browser, and pulled up his regular internet browser. He input the information into a maps website. The result could not have been any weirder — the cabin had sat on land that now was part of the Greensboro County Park. In particular, the Greensboro Science Center and Zoo covered every inch of those coordinates.

He heard water running from the bathroom upstairs. Rubbing his dry and heavy eyes, he crawled over to the couch. *Tomorrow,* he thought. He needed sleep, and then tomorrow — well, in a few hours anyway — he would make things right with Sandra and go visit the Science Center. Before he could think any further, his eyes closed and his conscious mind shut down.

Chapter 10

A DEEP RUMBLE VIBRATED IN MAX'S BELLY. His eyes creeped open. His neck had locked at an odd angle from sleeping on the couch, and as he rubbed the muscles loose, his brain noticed that the noise of the rumble had a name — garage door.

Sandra!

Adrenaline swept through his tired body enabling him to dash across the house toward the front door. He threw it open in time to see Sandra driving away.

"You've really ticked her off," Drummond said, rising up through the floor. "This might be a record."

Slinking into the kitchen, Max poured cold coffee into a mug and tossed it in the microwave for a minute. "We'll work it out. Marriages have fights. It's no big deal."

"Sure. If that's what you need to think in order to keep going."

Max slammed shut the utensil drawer. Holding a spoon like a shiv, he said, "I've been awake for less than two minutes. Let me drink my damn coffee."

Drifting into the study, Drummond looked over the pages of Max's notes that lay open on his desk. "Looks like you had a productive night."

After sipping coffee three times, Max closed his eyes and sighed. The crick in his neck hurt whenever he turned it to the left, but otherwise, he felt passable. "I don't know how productive it was, but at least I know more about the Mobley Coven. I figure this is all because of them hiring us, so the faster we finish the case, the faster we can put this behind us — get back to our lives."

"I'm not sure it's going to be that simple."

Ignoring the burn in his mouth, he downed a large gulp of coffee. "Give me a few minutes to clean up and then we'll go."

"Where to?"

"Greensboro Science Center. The Mobley Coven started somewhere near there."

Drummond's brow wrinkled. "Why there?"

"Can we please not play twenty questions just yet?" Max stomped upstairs for a short shower.

Fifteen minutes later, he sat behind the wheel and sped along Route 40 East towards Greensboro. The drive would take about forty minutes, and though he tried to play the radio and appear deep in concentration, he knew Drummond would use this time trapped in a car to discuss matters. Sure enough, the ghost appeared in the passenger seat, cleared his throat, and gestured to the radio.

When Max turned it off, Drummond said, "You and Sandra are my partners, so I got to know what's going on here. The two of you already fought it out about witches and all that. You were past this whole thing of having problems with her diving into it all. Why the sudden backtrack?"

"I'm not backtracking."

"Sure looks like it."

"If she wants to read and research the subject, I'm fine with it. I would never stand in her way of learning and studying anything. And I completely understand that when the subject is witchcraft, particularly the real thing that we have to deal with often, she might have to dabble a bit in practice. We've made good use of her spellwork, and I'm fine with that. But what's going on right now is something different."

"I don't see it. All she's doing is talking with witches. We all come into contact with real witches plenty. That's partly why I urged you not to take the case. But that's me. For you, why is it now a problem?"

"Because," Max said, gripping the wheel tighter, "we're married. We're husband and wife. And while it might've been different in your day, here and now it means that we work as a team. But she's not even trying to meet me halfway. Marriage is give and take. Except I give a little and she tries to take the whole thing."

"We're talking about Sandra here. She loves you."

"That's not in question. I know she loves me."

"Then why keep acting like a hardass?"

"Because I love her. This isn't right, and she refuses to let me have any say in the matter. In a marriage, though, no matter how big the decision impacts your life, no matter how much you think it's all about you, everything you do, every choice you make has a serious impact upon your spouse."

Drummond stayed quiet for a few miles. Then he pushed his hat back. "That's why you really took this case, isn't it? I mean I'm sure the money helped, but you figured you'd give her a little of what she wants."

"It was going to be a simple case. Missing person or dead person. That's it."

"You should've known better. Nothing is ever simple when dealing with witches."

"The thing is — we're in it now. I really need your help, your focus, your full commitment because if we don't get to the bottom of whatever is going on here —"

"Sandra could be in real trouble."

Max nodded. "If she gets too deeply involved with this coven ... I don't know."

"Okay, then." Drummond clapped his hands and rubbed them together. "Let's go."

Off the highway, Max made his way to Battleground Avenue, took a side street to Lawndale, and up to the Greensboro Science Center on the left, nestled in a clearing surrounded by trees. Three open tiers of parking flowed downhill from where the Center stood. Two school buses had parked at the bottom; otherwise, only a dozen or so cars were scattered about.

Before they entered the building, Max took the time to walk up and down each parking tier. He kept checking the tree line for the ruins of the old cabin. Without having to ask, Drummond dove into the ground and checked beneath Max's feet.

"Some old pipework, but no cabin and nothing indicating witchcraft," Drummond said.

"Let's go in."

After paying for his ticket, Max entered the building. From the outside, it looked like a mid-sized public school with a small courtyard out front. But inside, the place became larger. Still not huge, but they fit a lot into what space they had without it feeling crammed together. Quite a feat considering the Center consisted of an aquarium, an entire floor devoted to reptiles, a small museum, several miniature theaters, classrooms, robotics labs, and a zoo.

Standing in the lobby, Max saw the aquarium section went off to the right. He headed left toward the rest of the Center. The floor opened into a circle with a large pendulum used to demonstrate the turning of the Earth. It swung from a cable mounted above that reached straight down to the lower level below.

Off to one side near a gift shop and a café, stairs spiraled down around the pendulum. A mural had been painted on the surrounding wall that depicted a massive scene of snakes and monkeys in the trees, colorful parrots soaring by, a peacock on the ground as well as two tigers and more. Oddly, on the far side, a massive dinosaur had been painted into the scene.

"They're trying to fit everything in there," Drummond said.

Max decided they should start at the far end of the zoo section and work back towards the entrance. This section took up several acres in the back, behind the main building. Max had no illusions that he would find the meerkats perched upon the stone chimney of the Mobley Coven's old cabin, but he held onto the hope that they would uncover some evidence pointing toward the coven.

Following the winding path toward the tiger enclosure, Max's eyes roved across the wooded areas behind the zoo. Children dashed around while harried teachers and parent volunteers attempted to wrangle the kids into some semblance of order.

"When I was that age," Drummond said as he watched the rambunctious children, "I loved coming to the zoo. We didn't have computers, video games, or any of that. Seeing a real gibbon swinging around and flipping through air like a circus acrobat thrilled me."

"While you're enjoying memory lane, don't forget to look around for any sign of that cabin."

"About that." Drummond thrust his hands in his pockets and rocked on his heels — yet still floating through air enough to keep pace with Max. "What exactly is this going to do for us? Being out here and, if we succeed, finding this cabin?"

"Two things, really. One — what else can we do? We have no leads, nothing to go on, and Lena Mobley is either unable or unwilling to give us more information. Which leaves us with Two — since we have nothing to follow out there, I figure we should look into the people on the inside of this. Perhaps having the full story of the coven will enlighten our moves. If we're to find Candace Mobley, we could use a little light."

They strolled back along the path, passing lemurs, red pandas, wallabies, and howler monkeys. The ripe manure odor from the petting zoo wafted across their way and they circled back toward the beginning. Several times, Drummond dropped below ground. On each occasion, he returned shaking his head.

Max could see the frustration growing on his partner's pale face. Twice Max stopped to inspect what might have been an old board in the dirt or a piece of the cabin's roof. When these proved to be nothing more than a trick of the light on a log and a particularly flat rock, Drummond grunted his displeasure.

"What?" Max said. "You have something to say?"

A few passersby looked at him oddly, but nobody wanted to approach the crazy man.

Drummond said, "I'm not buying this. It doesn't make enough sense for us to be wasting time out here. I say this as your partner, as the guy who has your back and only wants the best for you — if you really believe the line you gave me, then we're in serious trouble."

"You saying I'm lying?"

"I'm saying that I think you're not working this case. I think you're trying to do what you can to investigate the coven as a means to getting into Sandra's business."

"She's my wife. Her business is my business. And if you've got a better idea on how to handle this case, I'm listening."

"That's just it. You've been up for hours now, and you've yet to ask me if I found anything about the Goodman hunters. Remember them? The people you asked me to look into?"

Max halted. How had he forgotten about them? He leaned on the wood fencing overlooking the giant tortoise exhibit and pored his focus on the enormous, lumbering creatures. If he dared look away, he would see Drummond's eyes and he would know that the ghost was right. But Max never intended to sidestep the case. Not consciously.

Floating up beside him, Drummond tilted back his Fedora and gazed at the animals. "It's okay. We all get a bit myopic at times."

"Myopic? That's a big word for you."

"I'll take your insult as acknowledgment that I'm correct. And, if it makes you feel any better, our time out here isn't exactly wasted. I kept expecting you to ask me about the Goodmans and when you didn't, I thought maybe you already knew, that maybe we came out here because you knew."

"Clearly, I didn't."

"You're allowed to be worried about her. I'm worried, too. But you can't go off the rails like this. That doesn't help anybody."

Max lowered his head and clenched his lips tight until he could swallow down the urge to yell. At length, with control, he said, "I am not *off the rails*. And I am not going to back off worrying about my wife. Sandra is smart and capable, and I give her all the credit in the world. But she's every bit as human as the rest of us. We can all be seduced into actions that we would never normally do. Ever since her interest in witchcraft became serious, I've kept an eye on the whole thing, and I'm telling you, she's dancing awfully close to the fire."

"So are you."

"What's that supposed to mean?"

"She's already mad at you for having PB spy on her. What do you think she'd do if she found out you were off here investigating her instead of the case?"

"That's not what this is." But part of Max now wondered if that was true. Turning back toward the building, he continued, "You said you found something on the Goodmans. What is it?"

Drummond hesitated, and for an instant, Max thought the ghost would refuse to follow him inside. But then Drummond drifted over. "It's possible that some of the members of the Goodman hunters are descendants from the original gang. Many of the men who formed the original group had gone on to do quite well in life, or in some cases, their kids built the family fortune. Nothing huge. Not Hull-type wealth. But respectable amounts that'd leave them all quite comfortable."

"Then they're a well-funded group."

"Definitely. But here's the kicker, the reason I thought you may have chosen this outing for a different purpose — as often happens with people who make large amounts of money, they start donating it to offset taxes. Several individuals in the group donated money right here, to the Greensboro Science Center. And before you dismiss it, I know lots of people donate here. But these are sizable donations. The kind that get you on a board of directors, and nearly the kind that gets your name on something."

They re-entered the main building and Max led them back toward the lobby. "How did you find this out? Looking up financial records doesn't seem like you."

"Course not. That'd drive me nuts. But I keep telling you that there are lots of ways to get information. You really need to build up your network of informants."

"I'm working on it."

"Well, work faster. Anyway, that's how I know. My contacts are good. And, frankly, it was on the strength of that information that I entertained coming out here with you. That cabin really was here, and something worthwhile must still be."

"You think those donations were like hush money? I suppose you're right. That kind of money brings with it access. And access means they'd be able to keep their eyes on whatever they sought."

Drummond shifted toward the wall, his face growing dark as his eyes narrowed on a man walking a few feet ahead. "Don't say anything else."

Max stayed quiet.

"Look at that man's arm."

As they walked toward the gift shops by the pendulum, Max eased toward the right so he could get a clear view. Drummond kept to the other side, not bothering to avoid people passing through him. Max already expected what he would see, and sure enough, when the man lifted his arm to scratch his head, Max spotted the same flaming cross tattoo they had seen in the abduction footage — the mark of the Goodman Witch Hunters.

Chapter 11

MAX'S PULSE QUICKENED as he followed the tattooed man through the winding halls of the Science Center. A gaggle of kids all wearing blue t-shirts rambled toward the zoo. They rushed by this tattooed man, a man capable of stealing another human being, a man who took part in murdering a woman because of her ability to study and learn how to manipulate Nature.

Sandra had taught Max that little fact — witchcraft was nothing more than rules that enabled the user to manipulate Nature. At the time, he thought she had oversimplified things. He still thought that, but tailing this murderer made him see her viewpoint a little clearer. Max had destroyed witches before, yet those situations threatened his own life or the life of the others. The idea that he might put together a posse and hunt down a woman he suspected might be a witch — that crossed a dark line.

Though Max kept quiet as they climbed downstairs, Drummond had no problem speaking. He knew only Max would hear him. "These fellas must regularly have members walking around here. Otherwise, the odds of us stumbling on one of them is too high."

Sort of, Max thought. He would have agreed if the man had been any other than the same man they had seen in the video.

"Then again," Drummond said, catching on to the same thought, "this guy being here, this specific guy, that says to me that he's here because of our case. Keep alert. Something's going down that has to do with the Mobley witches and the fact that their original house was on this land."

Only a few people meandered around the lower level. Max checked his watch — 1:12 pm. Most of the schools probably needed to pack up and take the kids home. The tattooed man walked along a straight hall.

The walls had been painted blue and several rooms had large glass panes for viewing. The rooms had long counters with terrariums lined up. Each one had a different environmental setting for the occupant — poison dart frogs, box turtles, cornsnakes, and such. It reminded Max of a science building at a college.

Halfway down the hall, they reached a T-junction. In the middle a large glass case displayed a stuffed eagle with its wings out wide. A fierce looking creature.

The man did not turn. Max hung back for a breath and then continued his pursuit.

"Max!" a voice called from behind.

Max turned around to see a mother calling out to her toddler. When he looked back, the man had disappeared.

Waving onward, Drummond zoomed ahead. At the far end, he turned to his right. Max hastened down the hall to follow.

He entered a dark, warm room with viewing windows set in cloth covered walls. In each window, he saw snakes. Big ones. Diamondback rattlers, cottonmouths, and coral snakes. Nasty, deadly creatures that would love nothing more than to get out of their boxes and roam around for a tasty morsel, maybe even have a bite of good ol' Max.

"This way," Drummond said from the other side of the room. When Max caught up with him, the ghost gestured to a door marked *Employees Only*. Winking, he said, "I assume you're okay with breaking that rule."

"Go follow the guy. I'll catch up."

Once Drummond slipped through the wall, Max peeked back across the room. He had broken into numerous places since beginning his career as a researcher and investigator, but never before did he commit those crimes in plain view. A few people gawked at the snakes. On the opposite side, a young girl pointed at a huge iguana. Nobody paid any attention his way. Trying to ignore the lump thickening in his chest, Max opened the door and walked in.

He entered a bland office room with stark florescent lighting. On a table to his left, he saw a large plastic tub filled with live rats.

"Hate to tell you this, boys, but you're snake food."

A short corridor linked to two other rooms that looked like any old office except for the occasional glass case with a lizard stuck to the side. Turning a corner, Max heard the jingle of keys. Drummond floated ahead, hovering near a door at the end.

"Come on, Max. This guy's opened a secret door. Really. It's fantastic. I mean, it's obviously just a door but you'd have to know about the hidden keyhole in order to unlock it. Plus, it slides into the wall instead of swinging out."

Max approached slowly, easing each footfall to avoid making noise.

Drummond poked his head back. With giddy pleasure, he said, "That secret door leads to secret stairs."

From behind, Max heard the *Employees Only* door open and a woman called out, "Derrick? You can't be leaving the door open." Footsteps approached.

Max opened the nearest door — a broom closet — and shot a quick motion at Drummond. "Go, go. Follow him. I'll be there soon."

"On my way." Drummond dropped through the floor.

Stepping between a mop bucket and wide push-broom, Max eased the door closed, leaving a sliver ajar so that he could watch the hall. A short-haired woman with broad hips and narrow shoulders crossed into Max's view. She swung a keychain attached to a tiny bungee cord.

"Derrick? You smoking again? You know you can't do that in here." She sniffed the air, then muttered to herself, "Where did that doofus go?"

Drummond shot straight up through the broom closet floor and stopped above the mop. "Hurry!"

"You're gonna kill me," Max snapped, his heart racing from the sudden jolt.

"Derrick?" The woman turned back down the hall.

"It's Candace," Drummond said. "She's down there and she's alive. Barely. You've got to get down there now."

"Do you see where I am?" Max knew he had spoken too loud even before the woman stopped near the closet door.

"Y-You better not be s-smoking in there."

She stared right at Max, but he knew she couldn't see him — not through that sliver of the open door. But she also would not be going away. Her hand lifted toward the knob and then fell back. Eventually, she would dismiss her fears and summon the courage to check the door. Max gave himself fifteen seconds at the most.

He thought about slamming the door open fast. He'd catch her off guard, scare her plenty, and knock her down, too. But unless he turned back and clocked her hard enough to rattle her head unconscious, she would be screaming for help in moments. Or worse, she might have the presence to rush back and call Security.

"Last chance, Derrick. If you're in there and you don't come out now, you'll be fired."

Max struggled for any plausible story he could tell her, but every scenario he envisioned ended up with him being kicked out, if not arrested. But as the woman put her hand on the doorknob, they both heard an awful howl — a terrible moaning like a wounded wolf.

With her hands quaking, the woman turned toward the sound, putting her back to the door. Max opened it slightly more, his own curiosity getting hold of him. Again, the sound echoed around them.

Max's jaw dropped. Drummond stepped into the hall carrying a large rattlesnake — probably two or three feet long. The woman could not see the pain wracking Drummond's face. She couldn't see the ghost at all. But what she did witness must have been a crushing terror — a rattlesnake floating through the air while a ghostly moan followed it.

She screamed, spun around, and tore off down the hall. The moment she left, Max popped out of the broom closet. Drummond dropped the snake, rubbing his sore hands against his sides.

"Don't let it go," Max said, backing away from the venomous snake.

"Relax. My touch is ice cold, so this guy is moving slow for the moment." Drummond tried to hide it, but Max could see that handling the snake had taken more out of him than expected.

Despite Drummond needing a breather, Max's situation had not changed. "I'm not taking a chance that when I try to walk by it, it doesn't suddenly warm up and decide it's pissed off at being held in the air."

"Stop being a child and get moving."

"You're the one making ghost moans. I didn't know you could do that."

"There's plenty about me that you don't know."

"Do you rattle chains, too?"

"Shut up and get moving. There were three Goodman hunters down there and it didn't look good for Candace."

The rattlesnake moved its head around in a lethargic circle. Its tongue flicked in and out as it tasted the air — no doubt, tasting the fearful stench from Max. He couldn't be sure, but Max swore the creature paused long enough to stare at him.

In the broom closet, Max saw a towel — stained and frayed but large enough to do the trick. He snatched it and took three hesitant steps forward. He tried to push out images of long, hooked fangs digging into his leg. A memory of a nature show popped to mind — some snakes could move lightening quick and lunge several feet forward.

He froze.

Was he already too close?

"Throw the towel already," Drummond said. "Or you can be the one to tell Sandra that we could have saved Candace's life, but you were held up by irrational fears."

"It's not irrational. That thing could probably kill me."

"Then throw the towel and save yourself."

The ghost had a point. Max held the towel out like a matador taunting a bull. But instead of shaking the cloth, he swung it forward and let it gently lay over the snake's head. The distinct sound of its rattle spoke loud and clear — it was not happy.

Max then grabbed the mop. He hurried ahead and when he reached the snake, he poked the towel with the mop, making sure to touch it away from himself. The rattlesnake snapped out at the mop, and Max let it go. As it clattered to the floor, he slipped behind the snake and hustled toward the secret stairs.

"Finally," Drummond said with a wink. "Glad you're okay." He pointed to a wall outlet next to a snack machine. "That's how you open it."

The outlet pulled out on a hinge. Inside, Max saw a keyhole and button. The keyhole had been turned to the side and the button glowed a promising green. Pressing the button set the hidden door sliding aside. Though low — Max would have to crouch in order to fit through — the door thankfully moved in silence.

Drummond waved him on. "Go. I haven't done anything like that in a while. Forgot how much it hurts. Go save Candace. I'll join you in a minute."

Max nodded and ducked in. Once on the other side, he stood at the head of a narrow staircase. Wiring, pipes, and wood framing pushed in, while four bare bulbs provided enough light that he wouldn't fall. Max hustled down the stairs.

The stairs and wall ended on the right. Max turned the corner.

He looked upon a brick garage with the now-familiar abduction van parked in the middle. A workbench with an overhead lamp and old tools had been set up against one wall. On the other side, in the empty bay next to the van, Candace Mobley hung upside down.

She had chains wrapped around her ankles, and beneath her head, the Goodman hunters had placed a metal tub of water. Around the tub, a crude casting circle had been drawn with chalk. They had her gagged — protection against her using the circle they planned to use against her.

The tattooed man stood next to her, staring at Max as he

entered. Max had made no attempt to silence his approach — thumping down wooden stairs made that difficult.

"I know who you are," the man said, "so I'm going to give you the courtesy of asking you to leave. We're on the same side, after all."

"I don't go hunting down people who don't cause trouble."

"Since when do witches not cause trouble? And they ain't people. They lost that right when they sold their souls."

"Sorry, pal, but you're operating on bad info. Witches don't sell their souls. At least, they don't have to. Come to think of it, I don't know who they'd sell them to. You know a buyer or something?"

To Max's dismay, the time for witty banter ended. He had hoped to drag it out long enough for Drummond to return. Instead, the tattooed man rushed forward.

Max set back into a fighting stance without even thinking. His martial arts training kicked in, and while he could not perform acrobatic acts of deadly grace, he could manage to hold his own — a rather new and welcome phenomenon as far as he considered it.

The tattooed man thought Max would be an easy beat-down, so he started with an intimidating right punch, swinging wide like a cowboy in a John Wayne flick. Max leaned back, letting the man's fist swish through the air, and returned with three sharp jabs to the ribs. He had to admit, he enjoyed the surprised look this earned.

Raising his fists like a boxer, the man took on a more cautious approach. He snapped out a few punches to get his distance and then moved in fast. He jabbed with his left, and while Max swatted it aside, the right followed through with the real strike. He nailed Max in the side and the painful blow reverberated straight through to Max's skull.

Coughing, Max bent over and put out his hand to hold off another attack. But the man refused to be gentlemanly — not that Max expected as much. In fact, Max hoped the man would attack because his intention had been a feint. As the man's tattooed arm arced overhead, Max used his position to place a firm back kick right into the man's gut.

As the man stumbled over, grabbing his stomach, Max stepped in a short half-circle, brought up his leg, and clobbered the man in the side of the head. The tattooed arm reached for the ground while the man groaned and wobbled. Good thing, too, because Max had used up his best, most reliable moves. Anything else might have resulted in failure and embarrassment.

"Well, well," Drummond said, dropping through the ceiling. "Looks like you're starting to finally understand how this business works."

"Hurry up before this guy gets moving again."

"Why don't you crack him in the head and knock him out?"

"Do you know what that really does to a person?"

"Makes it so they can't fight back."

"You can cause real brain damage, and I'm not going to sleep with that on my conscience — not when he's no longer a threat."

Drummond gazed at the tattooed man curled up on the floor. "We better hurry it up, then. He won't be down for long."

"That's what I said."

Ignoring Max's exasperation, Drummond strayed toward the workbench. "Looks like the chain connects over here."

Max did not move. He stared beyond Drummond at the two men standing in the back.

"Right," Drummond said. "I told you there were three of them."

Based on the wrench in one guy's hand and the baseball bat in the other's, Max guessed they did not have the same concerns about causing brain damage to him. He tried to recall anything he might have learned about fighting two men at once. All he could bring up was that they wouldn't attack one-at-a-time like in the movies. And his instructor's number one lesson about being in such fights — *don't get in them.*

The man with the wrench called out, "Terry? You okay?"

The tattooed man — Terry — grunted, and Max heard him

scuffling back to his feet. Standing still and getting beaten seemed like a dumb way to go out, so Max charged forward. Between a metal wrench and a wooden bat, he opted for the bat — he figured at least he had broken through wooden boards before.

As he dashed forward, the man pulled the bat back. Max leaped into the air and thrust out his foot in a flying sidekick. It shouldn't have worked, but the audacity of the move and Max's loud scream caused his opponent to hesitate. The kick landed on the man's side. The momentum of Max's entire body sent the man tumbling down.

"The brick," Terry yelled.

Max jumped to his feet and whirled around for the next attack. Terry's yell turned into a high-pitched cry and he dropped to the ground — the handiwork of Drummond's icy touch. The ghost held his head as he floated toward the ceiling. He'd be of no use for a few minutes. That left the metal wrench to deal with alone.

Except Max forgot that the man with baseball bat had only been knocked down, and Max had just committed the cardinal sin of fighting — *never turn your back on your opponent.* Even as the thought formed in his mind, Max felt the man's burly arms grab hold. He strained and struggled, but he would have had better luck freeing himself from a crocodile's jaws.

The man with the wrench walked up, made a fist, and punched Max in the gut. Max coughed out what little air he had in his lungs. He closed his eyes, knowing the next blow would be to the back of his head — and this time, the metal wrench would bring the damage.

But the blow never came.

The man with the wrench trudged across the garage and stopped at the far wall. Using the wrench, he scratched something into one of the bricks. Bright light flashed in a stuttering assault as if the paparazzi had shown up to photograph the garage.

When it ceased, spots filled Max's sight. With his arms still pinned behind him, he could not get free, but he could hear.

The sound would haunt him many times later in life. Cracking bone, a shrill scream, and a horrid sucking like a feeding baby — but not a human one.

As Max's sight returned, he saw a fist come straight into his gut again. The man with the wrench grabbed Max's shirt and yanked him back toward the stairs. Though finally free from the other guy's grip, Max had little strength left to fight. He tripped and the man tossed him forward.

"Check on Terry," the man said, and his partner laid down the baseball bat before hurrying to Terry's side.

Max crawled backwards until he felt the cool wall. To his right, the stairs leading back into the Science Center awaited, but he had no intention of breaking for it. Too weak. These men would catch him before he managed to get halfway up — and then they really would beat him badly.

The one hunched over Terry said, "He's not in good shape. Maybe he needs the hospital."

To Max, the other guy said, "If he needs the hospital, then so will you."

He stepped forward, and Max looked away. He didn't need to see the wrench coming down on him. Then his heart jumped.

Above, at the top of stairs, Max saw Sandra kneeling. She held her left hand at her shoulder, and in it, Max could see a stick of chalk. He had no idea how long she had been up there, but clearly it had been long enough to draw a casting circle.

Her eyes snapped open but she did not seem to be seeing anything. Then he heard two thuds. Looking back, Max saw that the two men had slumped onto the floor. Sandra gasped for air as she clung to the handrail for support.

Racing up the stairs, Max thrust out his arms. He swept her into an embrace and kissed her cheeks. Sweat soaked her body but after a moment, her breathing steadied and she smiled.

"You okay?" she asked.

"Me? What kind of spell took so much out of you?" He gazed down the stairs. "Those guys ... they're not ... I mean..."

Sandra raised an eyebrow. "You think I'd kill somebody?"

"To save my life, maybe."

She nodded. "For that, I probably would. But no. They'll wake up feeling horrible, but they'll be fine. It's really not that difficult a spell. I don't know why it hit me so hard."

"I do," Drummond called from the bottom of the stairs. "Come here."

Holding Sandra close, they climbed back down to the garage. Sandra covered her mouth when she saw the witch. The body looked much like the previous one — broken bones, emaciated and oddly discolored, the expression strained with pain. Max ushered his wife forward — no need to stare at that horror too long — until they caught up with Drummond.

"See that?" Drummond pointed to a single brick. Like before, this one had been scorched. "That's two. And this time we got to see what happened. That one fella wrote something into the brick and it burned like this. At the same moment, Candace Mobley suffered whatever you want to call what happened to her. There's a clear connection."

"What does it have to do with Sandra being wiped out by her spell?" Max asked.

"Because I experienced intense pain from holding that snake and touching Terry. I mean, far worse than normal. I should've been able to help you more both times, but I felt like I'd been clobbered by Tony Canzoneri."

"Who?"

"Welterweight champion in the early 1930s. How about Mike Tyson?"

"Yeah, I get it." To Sandra, he asked, "You know any spells like that?"

Wrenching her shoulder from under his arm, she stepped away. "Now you want my expertise. You're doing it again. You fight me and tell me you're so worried about me, yet the moment you need my help with witchcraft, you're happy to use me. What happened to you supporting me in all of this? What happened to me being the witch for our side?"

"It's not like that. I do want you to —"

"You know, we spent all those years telling ourselves we

needed to be honest with each other yet we'd always turn around and ignore what we said. We'd keep secrets. Now, we're doing it again about witchcraft. We go in these circles until it all becomes a big fight."

Drummond had moved closer to Candace's body. "Hey, you two, save your marriage spat for home. We've got work to do here."

Over his shoulder, Max said, "What now?"

"She's still alive."

Max and Sandra rushed over. The witch's eyes were two wide-open orbs. She turned her head toward Sandra and moaned a word. With as delicate a touch as possible, Sandra pulled off the gag. In a crackling whisper, Candace said, *"Black."*

"What's black?" Sandra asked. "What are you trying to say?"

With a scream, Candace cried out, *"BLACK!"* Her body jolted back and forth as her head snapped to the right with an audible crack. Max pulled Sandra back, but there was no need. Candace had finally died.

Max, Sandra, and Drummond did not move. They stared at each other in silence. Then Max's cellphone rang.

He jumped at the sound, and with a sheepish chuckle, he fished the phone from his pocket. The screen displayed a number but no name. "Hello?"

"Is this Mr. Max Porter?"

"Who is this?"

"I'm Jillian from Mount Tabor High School. We need you to come in right now to discuss PB's behavior. Principal Hardy is expecting you."

After ending the call, Max shook his head. Then, grabbing his sore stomach, he started to laugh.

Chapter 12

THE LAST TIME MAX SAT IN THE PRINCIPAL'S OFFICE, he had been caught smoking cigarettes in the boy's locker room with Jimbo Banker and Kenny Kisoto after fourth period. Back then, he feared the wrath of his mother. More, he loathed knowing that for years to come, she would reference this moment whenever she wanted to drive home her disappointment in him. That went on until he hit college and found better ways to disappoint her.

But now, sitting in a chair slightly less comfortable than a granite slab, watching Sandra's knee bounce fast enough to give a speed metal drummer a run, and with his own fingers tapping a similar rhythm, he saw things quite differently. His mother, no matter how angry she had been, must also have been terrified. Not of the principal, but rather of the idea that she may have failed as a parent.

Max and Sandra weren't even PB's legal guardians, yet Max found himself worried that all of his actions, no matter how good intentioned, may have contributed to ruining this kid and the chances he had for a decent future. But he pushed that idea away. PB had suffered hard times, yet he was far from ruined. The longer Max had to wait for Principal Hardy, the more convinced he became that this school had decided before the fact that PB was a bad seed and that Max and Sandra were the ones contributing to the boy's delinquency, sending him down a dark and dangerous path.

The small office felt hot, stifling. It closed in around him as if the drab walls looked down upon his concern and shook their head — *a good parent wouldn't be here,* they seemed to say. Phones rang from the main office beyond the thin door, people chattered away, students complained, yet in the Principal's office time stood still.

"You sent Drummond to look more into the Goodman hunters," Sandra said. "Smart move."

Max tried to hide his surprise. Was she extending an olive branch? "Thank you. I just want to say that —"

"You know what else is a smart move? Practically everything I've been doing. Interviewing the witches to get information about their lives and behaviors. Once they started opening up to me, I was able to find out about their fears, too. Amazing how when you treat them like human beings, instead of monsters with twisted minds, they actually talk with you. That's how I found out about the Goodman hunters myself and eventually found Laverne. That's also how I found out about the original Mobley cabin and figured out that they may have taken Candace there. And that's why I was in the right place at the right time to save your disloyal ass."

"Disloyal?"

She glanced back at the door to make sure nobody could hear. Leaning closer, her mouth a firm, angry line, she said, "You sent PB to spy on me. You don't trust me."

"I trust you completely. I also worry about you."

"Don't start that again. I'm sick of hearing it. Anytime you need an excuse for making the wrong decision about me, you claim it was all because you worried for my safety. But here's the real truth. Not too long ago, we had a case with the Darden family. Remember them? Young group of kids cursed into a house. Well, not really, but that was part of the lie they gave us. You had no problem calling me your witch at that time. You were all about how you've got your own witch, and you didn't have a problem with me sneaking upstairs in their house and casting spells."

"Because I trust you." He could feel his teeth gritting together. This looked bad. If Principal Hardy walked in soon, she would see what she expected — disharmonious parents who were doing a horrible job raising their boy.

"Saying you trust me doesn't make it so. Not when your actions show me the opposite."

Max opened his mouth, but he heard the click of heels. When the doorknob turned, he and Sandra sat with smiles plastered on their faces. He got up and put out his hand. "Principal Hardy, pleasure to meet you."

Carrying a coffee mug and a skeptic's grin, Principal Hardy looked like she had served in administration for too many years. Part of her probably yearned to get back into the classroom, while another yearned to be done with school altogether. Problem children like PB pushed her towards the latter.

She sat at her desk with a wearied sigh. "Good afternoon, Mr. Porter, Mrs. Porter. I'm sorry to have to call you in so soon."

"It does seem rather strange," Sandra said, her voice mellow and melodic as she overcompensated hiding her anger from moments before. "It's only the boy's first day. Unless you're going to tell me he set a student on fire, I can't imagine what he could have done."

Max looked sideways. "He didn't set anyone on fire, did he?"

"No," Principal Hardy said, her expression caught between an amused chuckle and a horrified gasp. "But he has had a rather difficult day adjusting."

"What does that mean?"

She opened a file folder and flipped through several pages. Max tried to understand how, after less than one full day, the school could have that many pages in a file on the boy.

"As I understand it," the principal said, "you are not actually his parents. Correct?"

Sandra crossed her legs and sat back. "We have an unusual situation. Both PB and Jammer J were homeless. We gave them work, so they could earn an income, and together, they rent an apartment. We had no idea how young they were until it was brought to our attention that they should be in school."

"I'm guessing you don't have any other children."

"Excuse me?"

"It's easier to tell ages when you've watched it happen in

front of your eyes."

Sandra paused, and Max inwardly cringed. She smiled harder. "Perhaps you're right. Regardless, we thought the boys should go to school, and Max's mother — she lives here and also helps with the boys — she brought them in and registered them."

"But neither you nor your husband nor your husband's mother, none of you are the legal guardians, correct?"

"The boys don't have any parents. But we're taking care of them."

"You understand I'll have to call Social Services. These boys will need to be put into foster homes so their well-being can be looked after and monitored."

Sandra sat forward. "We're the ones who got them off the streets."

"And that's commendable. But now it's time for them to get a more stable situation."

"You think we're not good enough, is that it? The boys want to be with us and we're happy to take care of them."

"Then why haven't you become their legal guardians?"

"Just because we didn't file the proper papers, you want to screw these boys even worse now? They've had a shit life. Their parents abandoned them. We're the only adults who've given them anything but pain, and you want to destroy that?"

"Of course not. I want what's best for these boys."

"Then why the hell are we here? Let them go to school and that's that."

"It's not so simple."

Max put his hand on the desk, trying to return a calm tone to the conversation. "We didn't realize that official guardianship was necessary. It never occurred to us, and that was our mistake. But we're happy to comply with whatever paperwork needs to be done and process the whole thing as fast as possible so that you are not in any trouble, no liability issues, or anything. If need be, we'll happily sign waivers of any sort to cover the school in the interim. But there's no need to pull the boys from their classes and uproot their lives again over paperwork."

Principal Hardy pinched her brow with two fingers. "J is a fine young man. He seems eager and happy to be here. If we were simply talking about him, I'd have no problem with keeping him in the school provided you went through the legal process."

"Great. Let's do that."

Sandra crossed her arms. In a dark tone, she said, "The problem, honey, is PB."

Clearing her throat, Principal Hardy said, "Yes, well, he is another matter. In this single day that he's been here, I have write-ups on PB — disruptive in class, uses inappropriate language, tried to bribe a teacher, propositioned several girls for sexual favors, and finally, he punched a student."

"He's had it rougher than J," Max said, not knowing if that were true. "And he's played the part of J's big brother for a long time. He's had to protect J from the ugly side of the world."

"That's part of the problem, too. On his own, J does remarkably well considering his limited education. But whenever the two boys are together, J's behavior diminishes rapidly."

Sandra glowered at the principal. "I see. Now you've decided that, through lack of good parenting on our part, PB is a bad influence on J and possibly the rest of the school. That about right?"

"I am not accusing you two of anything, and I don't want to fight."

"Then why did you call us in here and start insulting us?"

"That was not my intent." Principal Hardy grabbed a pen in a death grip. "I am sorry. My interest is only for the welfare and education of those boys. Can we agree that you share that same interest?"

"Of course I do. There's no need to be patronizing."

Hoping to pull things back from their teetering edge, Max said, "Perhaps we should discuss some ways to help PB adjust. Clearly we all were wrong to just throw him into a school day."

Principal Hardy said, "We're sorry about that. We didn't know he had such behavioral problems — however they came to be. And yes, we need to figure out a better way to acclimate him, but first, we have to deal with the consequences of today's behavior."

Sandra's fingers curled up. "We can deal with him at home."

"I'm afraid that won't be enough. Not until you're officially his legal guardians. And, frankly, he needs a hard lesson right away that bribing teachers and hitting students is unacceptable. I also think that this is an important moment to teach J that following PB's footsteps will only bring him trouble. So, both boys are hereby suspended for three days."

"What?"

"If, after that time, you can show that you have begun the process of taking legal guardianship of these boys, we'll allow J to return. At that time, we can discuss how best to ease PB into school society."

Bolting to her feet, Sandra thrust her finger at the principal. "Of all the crap I've ever seen, you are so full of it that the smell is turning my stomach. You dare to sit behind your little desk and condemn us as bad parents, you dare to say that we don't have the kids' best interests at heart, yet you want to go punish J for PB's behavior. Not to mention the idiotic lesson to a boy who resists going to school that if he misbehaves, he won't have to go school! Oh, you're batting a thousand, lady."

Max didn't know if he should stay seated, stand up, or run. With astounding self-control, Principal Hardy sipped her coffee before speaking in a soft voice. "While we've been chatting, the boys were brought to the office. They're waiting out by the front desk."

Sandra continued to flag her finger at the principal. "If you think I'll let this slide, you're gravely mistaken. I'll talk to the school board about this."

"I'm sure you will. You can get their number out front as you leave. But please remember that I'm trying to give everybody the best shot at success. If you'd rather not rise to the challenge, I can always call Social Services."

Max jumped to his feet and took hold of Sandra's hand before she lost complete control. They did not need to deal with her clocking the principal in the eye. "Thank you for your time. We'll get the paperwork started and see you in three days."

Escorting Sandra out to the front desk, Max thought he may have averted a catastrophe. Then he saw PB and J staring wide-eyed at them and wondered if a different catastrophe had begun. But PB smiled. Just a flash before he remembered to look ashamed. Enough to tell them that he appreciated Sandra fighting for him.

"Come on," Max said. "Back to the office. I still have plenty of work to do."

J handed a piece of paper that had all the official suspension information on it. Sandra stared at the yellow form as her tension abated. "Well, shit," she said and they left the school.

Chapter 13

IN RETROSPECT, Max should have called his mother and had her show up at the school, too. It would have been ugly, but it would have been far better than the new burst of fighting that erupted in their downtown office when Max and Sandra arrived with the boys.

After rehashing the principal's arguments — ones Mrs. Porter supported — she decided to open fresh wounds. "This is so typical. The two of you have no clue what you're doing, so instead of asking or learning, you just barrel on through it all."

Sandra stomped toward her desk. "We can't all be as subtle and gracious as you."

"If you'd been smart and kept your mouth shut, J would still be going to school tomorrow."

Max sat in his chair with his legs on the desk. He flipped open his laptop and checked his email. He wanted to do research, but he had to wait for the yelling to stop.

Drummond popped his head out of the bookshelf. "If you need a drink, feel free to grab the whiskey." Drummond had several hollowed out books that contained flasks of whiskey. Though the ghost couldn't drink it anymore, Max had kept them filled — originally as a gesture to his friend, but later as a necessity for his own uses. If the boys weren't in the room, he might have swung back a taste or two.

"J is learning a lesson, too," Sandra said, shooting a look at Max that dared him to make a comment. "He needs to make his own choices and not follow PB all the time."

J sat on the couch with his first-ever math homework on his lap. At first, Max thought J merely buried his head in work to avoid the fight — much like he did — but he could see the way J went over the problems and thought them out. When he finished one, checked the answer, and saw he was correct, a satisfied nod and a quick smile followed.

PB, on the other hand, watched the arguing adults closely. At length, he blurted out, "I didn't even want to go in the first place. Y'all think you get to decide about my life, but this is for me to do. I'm the one that's got to go every day."

Mrs. Porter blazed a glare at him. "And what do you plan to do? I'm assuming you've decided to cause trouble until you are no longer welcome at the school. Was that your brilliant plan? Because that's a child's plan. A real adult deals with problems. They don't run away."

"I'm not running."

"Sure looks it to me."

"Hey," Sandra said. "Don't belittle him."

"Oh, now you want to be a parent?"

Sandra's hand flattened at her side, and Max feared she would slap his mother. His stomach soured. Rarely had he seen either woman in such furious form.

Mrs. Porter went on, "Not only are the both of you clueless as to how the world works, but you honestly don't even see the trouble coming your way."

"We see far more of the world than most," Sandra said.

"Then why aren't you worried? Do you really think the school principal will risk her job to bend the rules for you? The only reason she said she wouldn't call Social Services was to get you two out of her office."

That caused everybody to pause.

In a less biting tone, Sandra said, "She promised she'd give us a few days to get things in order."

"Maybe she will, but I wouldn't put any money on it." To PB, Mrs. Porter added, "You see what you're causing? The State will come in and take you boys away. They'll throw you in separate foster homes and you'll probably never see us or each other again."

PB pounded his fist against the bathroom door. "They can't do that."

J kept his head down, but his pencil had stopped moving.

"They can and they will," Mrs. Porter said. "If we're lucky, this principal has a heart or at least the honor to stick by her word. But I don't put any faith in that. We'll have to wait and see if a social worker comes knocking on our doors."

Sandra said, "Will you stop terrifying these kids?"

"I'm giving them the truth."

"Really? Because you don't know for a fact any of that is happening. If the principal wanted to call in Social Services, she would have done so while we were in her office — or before we even showed up. No way would she have allowed PB and J to come home with us."

"Now you're an expert on Social Services?"

And the fighting continued. Max closed his laptop, grabbed his coat, and headed for the door.

"Where do you think you're going?"

He couldn't tell whether that was his mother or his wife. Didn't matter, though. His answer was the same. "We've still got a case to work. So, before they cancel their check, I'm going to the library and getting some work done. You two can fight all night, but it won't change anything here."

Max left, making sure to close the door before either of them could retort. He hustled down the hall, down the stairs, and down the street until he reached his car. Once he pulled into traffic, he could feel his pulse slacken. He still heard the arguments in his head, still worried about what the world had waiting for the boys, but by the time he reached Wake Forest University, he had calmed his mind enough to focus on research. He parked and walked toward the Z. Smith Reynolds Library — ol' reliable.

Often when he entered this sanctuary of knowledge, he allowed himself a few moments to enjoy the architecture — two separate buildings brought together by turning the alley between them into a sky-lit, open air workspace. The former outer-walls became balconies overlooking the numerous tables on the carpeted floor, and all around, students had their heads buried in books, computers, and phones.

Max chose a table in the back corner and set up his laptop.

Next to that, he opened a notebook — some old habits die hard — and he wrote *Black* at the top. Candace's final word hopefully meant something.

But what to search for?

His still fingers rested on the keyboard. The word *Black* would bring up endless hits about everything from the color itself to racial discussions to an album by Metallica. None of which would help.

However, the word came from a witch, and for witches, colors held specific meanings. Color in relation to witchcraft also created different results — blue candles, white candles, every color candle changed the results of a spell. Even black.

In the search bar, Max typed: *color black and witchcraft*. After clicking on several links, and avoiding the more obvious references to black magic, he found enough similar information stating that black symbolized negation, canceling, unburdening, and most interestingly, the breaking of curses. Though he did not feel strongly about this avenue of research, he decided to delve a little deeper.

I could call my wife. Except Max knew he would not. The idea of asking her to look into witchcraft would have been foolhardy at any time lately, but under the current circumstances and right after he left her to fight with his mother — that would be suicidal.

After nearly thirty minutes of combing through witchcraft websites, however, Max had to admit that either he needed Sandra to point the way or that he had taken a wrong turn. He had learned that by the "old Earth code" of witchcraft, the color black centered in the feet and associated with reflection. Mirrors were a big deal, too. Then other sites suggested that the color black meant the canceling of reflections, but perhaps that was part of the "new Earth code," if they even called it that.

He made a note that he would have to ask Sandra at some point, yet he did not feel confident any of it mattered. Research, by definition, meant taking wrong turns at times, and this had all the hallmarks of a wrong turn.

"Then it's back to the start," he said to the screen.

He typed: *black and north carolina.* As expected, the results crossed a wide spectrum — Black City, Black Mountain, African Americans in North Carolina, articles on black culture in the South and in North Carolina, Black laws of 1844, the Woolworth Lunch Counter protest, and much more. Max was fishing for a morsel that might stick, but he saw little that made him think Candace had been referring to anything on his screen.

This was her dying word — *black*. After all she had suffered, why would she waste her breath when the people who had come to save her had finally arrived? She wouldn't. She must have been trying to communicate something of value with them.

Again, he went back to the search bar: *black and goodman witch hunters*. This brought up nothing useful, especially considering the top hit referred to an article titled, "Is actor John Goodman secretly black?"

Leaning his chair back, he gazed up at the skylights several stories above. He knew nothing about Candace. Once again, he recognized that Sandra, having interviewed several witches, might have provided some answers to that mystery — another thing he would have to ask her about later. He knew both Candace and Laverne had suffered a horrible death, but he had no good way of searching for information on the kind of spell involved — not without Sandra's help. She had the books that wouldn't be available on the internet, many not even on the darknet. He knew that the Mobley Coven had been marked by the Goodman hunters, but like all else in this case, both groups worked at keeping themselves out of the history books and the public record — as much as possible.

The bricks.

That was an odd bit in this case. Odder than the usual level of odd for their cases. Spells, casting circles, secret rooms, and murder — Max had experienced these things before. But the bricks — that was new.

Assuming the word *black* truly held importance and that it had some connection to the spell, then perhaps he needed to add the bricks into his thought process. Sitting forward, he returned to the search bar and typed: *brick spells and black.* Nothing.

Max scrolled through links to many of the sites he had visited before. He saw reference to many of the same conspiracy theories and New Age hypotheses, none of which would help him out. But three pages into the results, he read something that made him stop — a link to *George Black, North Carolina Master of Brick Making.*

All of Max's researching neurons fired off. His skin tingled. His pulse picked up and he could not hold back a satisfied smile. George Black. This was what he had been looking for. It had to be.

But before he could click on the link and begin his exploration, a firm hand rested on his shoulder. An older gentleman lowered his strong-featured, dark-skinned face and read the name on the screen. Max didn't have to look. He knew exactly who stood next to him. Leon Moore — right hand of Mother Hope.

"Max, I hope you'll trust me when I say that it is best you leave this alone."

Chapter 14

LEON PULLED BACK A CHAIR at the table, gestured to it, and raised his eyebrows. Max nodded and Leon sat. Not that his nod mattered. Leon would have sat anyway. But the moment of polite manners brought a sense of civility to the situation — one which Max thought far from civil.

"Let me state this in clear terms," Leon said. "I don't want there to be any confusion or mistakes." Working for the leader of the Magi had given Leon access to a lot of power, and in one way, he always took advantage — despite being an elderly man with a bad back, Leon looked to be in his early-sixties, strong and vibrant. Even some of his hair had grown back and it had returned a lush black instead of dirty gray.

Max closed his notebook and shut down his laptop. "My arrangement with Mother Hope allows me to take on cases outside of the Magi group. You shouldn't be here telling me I can't investigate a case."

"Not all cases are the same. You've stumbled into a mess that I hope to get you out of, but in order to do that, I need you to stop looking into these things."

"What things? I don't even know what I've been looking into."

"You know enough to recognize that your arrangement with Mother Hope goes only so far. That the cases you take on mustn't interfere or conflict with Mother Hope's interests."

"And this one does?"

"It involves witches. What do you think? And another thing — I strongly suggest you dissuade your wife from furthering her knowledge of witchcraft."

With a scoffing chuckle, Max said, "Isn't your job to know all about us Porters? Because if you're seriously asking me to influence Sandra like that, then you don't know crap about us." Max put away the last of his things and stood. "You've delivered your message. I got it — stay off this case. Go back to your witch and tell her you were a good dog. But don't expect gratitude or graciousness from us. The only reason I still do anything for Mother Hope is because she has me cursed, and I don't want to ever see the full extent of what that thing can do." Thinking about the curse caused the mark on his chest to heat up. "Anything else?"

With a sharp crack to his voice, Leon said, "Sit down."

Max did not move.

Like a parent fed up trying to rein in his temper with a disobedient toddler, Leon said, "I have a few things more to say. Please, have a seat."

Nothing good would come from pissing the man off further. Max had made his point. He sat.

"Thank you," Leon said. He paused and set his elbows on the table as he hunched forward. "I know your hostility towards myself and Mother Hope has some justification."

"Some?"

"Right now, the thing I'm asking of you, this is for your own protection. I'm trying to look out for you and your wife."

"Yet I felt much safer before you started talking to me."

Cracking his knuckles, Leon said, "If you'll stop with the jokes, I've got something important to tell you. Something that might change the way this whole town runs. See here — I know from the outside it looks like all is settled and strong for us. But it ain't so. Mother Hope learned real fast that it's one thing to complain about those in charge, but it's much harder to actually be one of those in charge. It's easy to find fault with how things are run, but when you've got to make all the decisions, running things ain't so easy."

"Mother Hope's having a little buyer's remorse now that she got rid of the Hulls. That it?"

"I think the pressure of being the sole decision-maker is becoming a burden to her." Leon scowled. "No. That's not right. I can't sugar-coat this. More and more, her reactions to the daily problems that need solving — well, they're not always rational."

"I'm not making a joke with this, but when has she ever been rational? She's a witch. I know you all like to play the card that you're the good guys, that you want to hold all the power to make sure people don't abuse magic. That sounds noble and all, but since you're apparently having a bout of honesty at the moment, let me be honest. No matter the intentions, your group is trying to take the throne that the Hulls were kicked off."

"I'd say we already took it."

"If so, you're being awful quiet about it. Plenty of witches out there doing what they want, free of any of the restrictions they once worried about."

"You didn't really expect us to run things in the same ham-fisted way the Hulls did."

"No, but for all Mother Hope's talk of keeping the peace and protecting people from witchcraft, well, I expected to see a drop in my witch-related caseload. That hasn't really happened."

"You're side-tracking me. The thing I want you to focus on, the point here, is that our leader may no longer be able to make good decisions. In fact, I think she's starting to make dangerous decisions."

Max absently rubbed his chest. "How long has this been going on?"

"Long. Probably started a few months after the Devil's Tramping Ground."

"Are you serious?" It was at the Devil's Tramping Ground that all the major players faced off. It was there that the Hulls met their fate and the path for Mother Hope to gain control opened up. For corruption to set in so fast left Max wondering if anybody could hold that position and stay sane.

Leon glanced around before speaking again. "I want to be very clear. I am not betraying Mother Hope. I am not telling you that she's unstable or in trouble."

"You sure? Because it sounds like that's exactly what you're telling me."

"I still believe in the Magi's mission, and I still believe that Mother Hope is the witch we need to be in charge. Transitioning to such a level of power, especially when the previous rulers left nothing behind to guide the way, is bound to cause lapses in judgment and other conflicts. In the long run, I know Mother Hope will pull through, and she will bring us to an era of peaceful existence with the rest of the world." Before Max could toss in another comment, Leon leveled a chilling glare. "Despite our past — yours and mine — despite what you may think of me, I do care about you and your lovely wife. I don't want to see harm come to you. That's why I came here. I'm warning you to stay off this case. Mother Hope is not well right now, and I can't promise she won't do something drastic if she finds out what you're up to."

Max threw his hands up. "I don't even know what I'm up to. Why don't you tell me, so I know what to avoid? That'd be some real help."

Leon stood. "If you haven't figured it out yet, so much the better. Walk away from it all right now and you'll never have to be bothered with finding out."

"Really? You think that's the way to turn me away? At least give me a hint of something."

"I've done what I dare." Ignoring Max's further attempts to grab a little information, Leon walked away.

Max did not bother getting up. He knew Leon would say nothing more. Most of his protest, begging, and joking served only to entertain himself. After all, how could Leon expect Max to listen to anything coming from the people who cursed him?

On the other hand, the fact that Leon felt it necessary to warn Max off the case served as confirmation that the Porters were getting closer to a real answer. All of which suggested that they needed to go back to the original source and ask some tough questions. Especially about ...

Max's face brightened. He grabbed his cellphone and called Sandra. After quickly telling her about Leon, he said, "Meet me at the Mobley house. And bring Drummond."

"Sure. What exactly are we up to?"

"We've been turning over every rock we could to find out what's going on here. It's time to turn over the biggest rock of all. We're going to find out what's behind that door they've got warded off."

Chapter 15

WHILE MAX AND SANDRA SAT ON THE COUCH in the living room of the Mobley house and Lena Mobley sat in the high-backed chair opposite them, Drummond hovered against the wall with his hat low and mood lower. "I'm going on the record here saying this is a bad idea. Maybe even stupid."

Max grinned as he pushed the yammering voice from his head so that he could focus on the matters in front of him — namely, Lena Mobley. "Thank you for seeing us again."

"I take it this concerns Candace," Lena said.

The death of Laverne had clearly hit her hard. Max worried what their current news would bring. Drummond had said as much on the drive over, pointing out that breaking into a room the witches obviously wanted kept private would have been a bad idea under any circumstances, but doing so while the witches in question suffered losses screamed of a death wish.

"Especially," Drummond had said, "when I can't help you because I'm the very thing they got that door warded against."

Lena pulled a handkerchief from her pocket and dabbed at her eyes. "It's okay. You don't have to say the words. I know she's dead. I knew it the moment it happened."

"You did?" Sandra sounded more amazed than alarmed.

"We sisters have a bond stronger than most can comprehend. It stretches beyond the corporeal world. We can feel and hear and sense much about each other. It's one of the many gifts that comes when you join a coven."

Max didn't know if he believed any of what she said, but he could see that Sandra wanted to believe it all. He coughed to break the gaze between the two women. "We're sorry we failed again. That's not how we do things. But it would have helped if you had been upfront with us."

"I told you all I could."

"You didn't mention the name Black."

She shrugged. "I don't know anybody by that name."

"I'm sure. Here's the problem. We don't believe this is going to end. Your coven has been targeted by an old witch hunting group. They will come again unless you help us with the information we need to stop this."

Drummond paced the air above. "It's not too late. Conduct this like a normal interview, try to get a solid lead, and get out of here."

Lena pulled her lips in tight. "We didn't hire you to play vigilante. We wanted Laverne found, and you did that. We wanted Candace found, and you did that. Let us consider your efforts successful within the confines of what we paid for. We won't be needing you anymore."

"Until the next one of you goes missing. Maybe it'll be you. Or that young gal — what was her name? Jessica?"

"I think you better go."

Sandra put out a placating hand. Max felt a twinge of pride — even with the two of them fighting, she could still come through for him. She said, "Please, Ms. Lena, this has been a difficult case for us. Not difficult to fulfill, but difficult to witness the harm that came to your sweet sisters. We don't want that to happen again, and frankly, I doubt you want it to happen, either. My husband's blunt words are merely a reflection of the urgency we feel in your case."

"I see." Lena scooted her back straighter against her chair. "In that case, thank you for your concern."

"Perhaps if we all had some tea or coffee and discussed the case, maybe we can find a way to satisfy everybody involved. Surely we can manage to protect you and your sisters, put a stop to this danger, without encroaching on your inner-world. Especially now that we know who we are dealing with."

"Perhaps." Lena thought for a few seconds. "Is coffee okay?"

"That'd be perfect."

Once Lena left the room, Drummond dropped by the

kitchen door. "I'm participating because you two are my partners, but don't think for a second that I approve."

As Max and Sandra headed for the stairs, Max said, "You only disapprove because you can't jump into the room and help us."

"I don't approve because these witches are being much too nice to you. There's something ugly going on here and I don't think you should dig into it too much. Besides, I like to have fun, too. Why should you two get to do all the sneaking around on this one?"

Max led the way upstairs, trusting that Drummond would do his part despite his complaints. At the top, Max spied a hall with several doors. Nothing surprising there. The first door on the right opened into a bathroom. The opposite door was locked.

As Sandra approached, Max said, "No way is it this one. Let's move on."

Sandra eyed the door, shrugged, and followed Max. The rest of the doors opened into bedrooms and a closet. "Strange," Sandra said. "Seemed like it had to be one of these."

"Let's try that locked door."

"Of course. We should have done that first."

They hurried to the locked door and Max tried the knob. "Nope. Won't open. Maybe we're wrong and there's nothing to do up here."

"Maybe," Sandra said, but she frowned.

"What's wrong?"

"I don't know. Something seems off."

"Let's go back downstairs and check on Drummond. It's going to hurt him if he has to hold that kitchen door closed and maybe he can clue us into whatever he saw up here that bothered him so much."

"Good idea."

Halfway down the stairs, they stopped. "What are we doing?" Max said.

Sandra gazed up and smacked her forehead. "We've been hitting a ward against people. Makes us unable to see the door as our goal."

"Warded against ghosts and people?"

"More than one ward. Probably a few others, too."

Lena walked to the stairs. "Most definitely." She did not look pleased. "Your ghost has been sent to the Other. I don't think he'll be returning anytime soon. As for you two, the Mobley Coven did not gain all its power to be subverted by a couple of weak amateurs."

"Sticks and stones, lady," Max said, though he did not feel as defiant as he fronted.

Lena's glower sent shivers through Max's bones. "I'm surprised that you tried what you did. We paid you well — even after you botched both jobs — and all we wanted was for you to turn away from it now. Instead, you betrayed us."

"I'm sure you do see it that way. From our side, I see it that you did pay us well but you neglected to tell us most of the truth. We failed because of that. You let that sink in. Your two sisters would be alive if you had simply told us the truth."

"Not so simple."

"That's what most liars say." He clasped his hands behind his back to hide their shaking. "Now, it's obvious that you don't want us around. Seems like nobody does. So, if you'll step aside, we'll leave and won't bother you again. At least, not until your neglect crashes into the rest of what we deal with. But then, you won't care about that, will you?" He hadn't meant to throw that last verbal jab and regretted it the second the words shot from his mouth.

Lena's eyes fired up. "You —"

But she didn't get any further. A loud click echoed throughout the house. Lena's eyes snapped upward. The long creak of a rusty door followed. Max and Sandra pivoted to view the landing at the top of the stairs. Nobody stood there, but Lena gazed upon that empty space with fear.

"Lena, dear," a voice crackled like brittle bones. "It's okay. I want to talk with them."

Bowing, Lena said, "Yes, ma'am." She climbed the stairs until she stood above Max and Sandra. Without looking back, she said, "Follow me."

Leading the way, Lena headed to the bedroom at the end of the hall. She opened a bureau drawer and removed a journal. With a disgusted huff, she ripped a page from the book — one on which Max snatched a peek of archaic symbols. When she turned back, she looked Max up and down. "You better be worth this."

Sandra whispered to Max, "That ward must have taken hours to cast."

Lena brushed by and escorted them to the locked door. It now stood ajar. As they stepped in, Max realized that the powerful ward had prevented him from even looking inside when they had passed by only moments ago.

The room they entered spoke to an age long gone. Heavy maroon curtains blocked most of the outside. A large fireplace burned two logs, stifling the room with a wall of heat. Two chairs, a four-poster bed, and two end tables — all dark mahogany. Oversized oil paintings weighed down the walls. And in the center of it all, propped up against four enormous pillows with dark casings, Max saw the hollowed out eyes of a witch.

His stomach turned.

Her sunken face and mottled skin looked horrid. One eye had clouded a milky white. The witch's stark hair, as white as her eye, dribbled across the pillows. She could not have weighed more than ninety pounds, and Max found it difficult to discern the outline of her body amongst the wrinkles of the bedding. If he had not seen the other afflicted witches already, he would have assumed she suffered from anorexia or some related condition. A sour odor lifted from her withered form that could not be masked by the three sticks of burning incense.

While Max and Sandra stared in shock, Lena moved into the side bathroom and returned with a clear bag. She bent to the side of the bed and carefully switched out the old witch's colostomy bag. As Lena cared for the old woman's medical maintenance, she nodded toward the chairs.

Max and Sandra sat. When Lena finished and had removed the full bag to the bathroom, she said to the old woman, "Are you sure?"

"I am," the woman said, her voice a series of snapping clicks that forced Max to shudder.

Lena nodded. "Mr. and Mrs. Porter, allow me to introduce Grandma Mobley. You might know her as Eunice Mobley, the founder of our coven."

Chapter 16

MAX AND SANDRA DID NOT MOVE. Though the sight of the woman disturbed him and her voice caused an unsettling involuntary response, Max showed no surprise at her identity. He did not need to look at Sandra to know she also remained calm.

Lena, however, did not appreciate their relaxed attitude. "Do you not believe me?"

"We do," Max said.

"This is Eunice Mobley. Born in 1877. She's nearly a hundred and fifty years old."

"We understand. We've met people far older, though, so let's get on with this. I have a hunch that a lot of the pieces are about to fall into place." Raising his voice, he said, "Isn't that right, Grandma Mobley?"

Under great strain, she lifted her hand to briefly touch Lena. Her fingers poked out at odd angles from arthritis and possibly breaking numerous times. Max studied the woman's face, finding it hard to equate what he saw with the vivacious, defiant woman from the photograph of Eunice Mobley with three unidentified women in front of a barn.

"Yes," Lena said. "You wanted the full story, the truth of what's going on, then so be it. But remember, you are still working for us. We paid you a lot of money, and you chose not to walk away from us. We now expect you to see things through."

"You say that like we had a choice. The moment we agreed to take on the case, we knew we would have to see it to the end."

"My, aren't you a noble bunch."

Sandra snorted a laugh. "Not at all. But we learned long ago that the best way to deal with all of our cases was to push right on through until it ended."

"Let's start that pushing now," Max said. "You have something to tell us."

Lena lowered onto the edge of the bed. She reached out and laced her fingers in the crooked bones of Grandma Mobley's hand. "Very well. I won't bother with the early years of her life. If you are half as good a researcher as I have been told, you can find out such details later."

"I already know that part. You want to pick up when she moved to Greensboro. Perhaps around 1920?"

Lena sneered at his cockiness. "1917. A few years before, Eunice had been, more or less, evicted from Winston-Salem, and rather than risk facing the same from the locals in Greensboro, she chose to live in a small cabin off in the woods to the north of the city. Of course, people still came to her, seeking out her services even as they decried her existence, happy to pay her anything for her spellwork, but equally happy to hang her for the same if they got found out.

"Despite this, despite the precarious life of a witch, despite the bigotry and hatred and all the evils perpetrated against our kind, Eunice persisted. She did not want to die. She loved life. More than most. She reveled in all its wonderful beauty and charm. She was a free spirit, a progressive woman in a regressive world, simply waiting for society to catch up with her."

Max thought of the way the town had distrusted her and of the strange deaths that had surrounded her. "I thought you were going to tell the truth. Eunice was not some carefree peace-loving guru whose only crime was being misunderstood. She liked to play on the dark side of things, didn't she?"

Bristling, Lena said, "You obviously need to learn more from your wife. Witches are many things, and while we do skirt the edges of powerful forces, we also can love, laugh, and thoroughly enjoy life. Why do you think most of us get involved in this? Our lives are enriched, strengthened. We are filled with excitement and power. We get to truly live, and for most, we wish all women could join us."

"You're like an ultra-feminist movement."

"Only if we take over the world." She grinned, and Max could not tell if she meant to be taken seriously or not.

Sandra pinched Max's leg to shut him up. "Please continue."

"Eunice is a smart woman — one of the most ingenious minds I've ever encountered. Back then, she realized that a day would come, far in the future, when our kind would not have to hide, when our power would no longer be used for parlor tricks or to help desperate souls willing to risk the scary forest to find the lone cabin. A day would come when we could sit amongst the wealthy and strong, and we could influence our world in a significant way.

"She understood this future awaited our kind, yet she also understood that she would not live long enough to see it. Unless ..."

Sandra stepped over to the bed and intently inspected Grandma Mobley's skin. "The only spells we've ever come across that can let a person live inordinately long are curses."

"Indeed. But this is no curse — not in the way you mean."

Returning to her seat, Sandra said, "A spell gone wrong?"

"There are no good spells to let you live eternally. If there were, you'd have thousands of witches, each hundreds of years old, still walking around. Now, Eunice did not know many witches back then, and amongst those she did know, she was the most advanced. She began studying her books, searching for a good spell, but as I have said, she only found curses. She considered a Call to Power, but that seemed a poor substitute since it still meant dying. Her strength, her power, would be transferred to another, but that did not appeal to her." A squeeze from the twisted hand and Lena chuckled. "I know, Grandma. It still doesn't appeal to you.

"But in 1917, she read the book that would change her life and ours. It was call *The Book Beyond,* and it had been rumored that it held one of the darkest secrets to be found anywhere — something so profound that it could only be read once or the student would go insane."

Sandra straightened. "I've read about a book like that, but it was called *The Forever Book*."

"It's had many names. Don't bother searching for it. She had the only copy and when she cast the single spell within it, the book was destroyed. It consumed itself."

Grandma Mobley coughed, a feeble sound that still managed to threaten to break the last of her intact bones. In her sandpaper voice, she said, "I don't want any other lips to say his name. I've dealt with the consequences, but too many have paid my price as well."

"We love you," Lena said. "No price is too high."

"Sweet child, I love all my sisters, too. But allow me this. His name was Mr. Dahlston."

Before Max could repeat the name, Sandra grabbed his hand and shook her head. "This is a name that you should never say in the company of the witch that cast the spell in that book. To do so, will call him upon us."

Max wrinkled his forehead. "But she just said it."

"That's because he's always with her. She can sing his name all day long, it won't make him jump to her again. He's already there, watching her, watching his investment. But if you or I said that name, he would take form, ready to strike a deal. And he's not one to walk away without his deal made."

Lena tilted her head. "You have been reading about all of this. I'm impressed."

"What is all this?" Max said. "Are you saying she sold her soul to the Devil?"

"Don't be ridiculous. There is no Devil — not in the sense you mean. Here is what happened: After casting the spell, the gentleman in question arrived at her cabin door. He is not the Devil nor a demon nor any such ridiculous thing. But he is a powerful being, once a man, who lost himself inside the darkness of dark magic. That book, *The Book Beyond*, he created it as a calling card of sorts. He found ways to prolong life — ways that are far superior and more reliable than the trinkets Mother Hope uses or the curses others foist upon their victims. This man, for lack of a better explanation, is an agent of Evil incarnate, and he's always happy to make a deal for that power."

"*Evil incarnate?* I hate to play the skeptic, especially because we have seen a lot of weird crap in our time here, but I'm having trouble believing this." To Sandra, he asked, "Is this possible?"

Sandra said, "From what I've read, that was the purpose of the spell. It took all the evil energy surrounding the casting circle and brought it together in a human form. Probably required a cadaver to possess. But it's not like evil is actually a living, breathing being. This spell within that book simply gave that energy temporary form."

"A form that can make deals?"

"Hon, you speak to a ghost all the time. What do you think he is? What do you think a soul is? It's all about forms of energy."

"It should be quite clear now," Lena continued, "that Grandma Mobley wanted to live forever, wanted to build a coven that would be the strongest of all, wanted to see the world change so that our kind could live in the open. The man promised he could fulfill that request, and of course, the question on her mind was obvious."

"What's it going to cost?"

"Exactly. A being composed of evil energy has no interest in material goods. It lives off further energy. Mr. Porter, you want to know why many witches do evil things — it is because sometimes that's the price required for the things we seek."

"Wait a second," Max said, failing to keep the ridicule from his face. "Are you trying to suggest that the only reason your coven of witches has ever done anything remotely wrong or evil is because you've been paying the debt of dear, sweet Grandma Mobley? You really want me to swallow that?"

"I don't care what you choose to believe. This is what I believe, and you wanted our story. This is how I know it to be. Besides, that truth only lasted a few decades. Eventually, our own suffering would be required to satiate the man."

Sandra said, "Why are you suffering?"

Stroking the back of Grandma Mobley's hand, Lena said, "After the deal was made, the evil man told Grandma Mobley that she must pick a vessel for her spirit. It would reside in this vessel until the day came when she failed to satisfy the man's need for energy."

"Clever. As long as you continue to do evil acts, then Mr. Evil gets what he wants while your matriarch and your coven continue to exist."

"Except we were promised more than mere existing," Lena snapped. Grandma Mobley lifted one finger and that proved more than enough to calm Lena. "I apologize for my outburst. Well, the time had come and at that moment, Grandma Mobley — Eunice — arrived at a bright solution. Whereas most witches would have named something precious to them or something they thought they could hold onto, Eunice understood that the easier the object was for the man to hold, the easier it would be for him to betray her, control her, or manipulate her — and, down the road, betray, control, or manipulate the coven. So, she pointed to the red clay beneath her feet and named it. All of North Carolina is covered in the dense clay, and she expected her spirit would be dispersed throughout."

Max listened to the struggling breaths of the old witch. "Let me guess. It didn't work out that way. The man feeding off evil betrayed you anyway."

"He did. But like all deals of this nature, his betrayal did not break the bonds of the spell for he kept to the spirit of the deal. You see, just because Eunice expected her soul to be spread thinly throughout all the red clay of North Carolina, the man instead placed it within a relatively narrow radius of the cabin."

Max jolted in his seat. "The bricks. That's what this is about."

"Red clay is one of the key components of a brick, and in North Carolina, for a time, brick-making was big business. As the decades went by, the coven came to be, we grew stronger and more influential, and we moved to Winston-Salem. At the time, Grandma Mobley had no idea her plan had been thwarted. But since then, it has become clear that her spirit has been imprisoned in several of the bricks throughout Winston-Salem. We have spent years searching for them yet have found none outside our city.

"We were content to leave it as such. Whether the clay lay dormant in the ground or baked into the walls of a building did not matter."

"Until you all started dying," Max said. "Hold on. Why is this hurting the coven and not just Grandma Mobley?"

"As part of our initiation into the coven, we ingested some of the red clay, made it part of ourselves, knowing that her spirit would bond with our own. So, we are all bound together."

Sandra said, "And with each brick destroyed, one of you is destroyed as well. Along with part of Grandma Mobley."

"When we are gone, she will be all that's left. We don't know if the man will kill her then or if he will force her to live on, suffering in eternal torment."

Max asked, "Why don't you just grab the bricks and put them somewhere safe?"

"We don't know where they all are, for one."

"Do you know how many there are? If your spirits are tied up with the clay, then there could be one for each of you. You could be diffused over hundreds of them, or —"

"Two."

"Two?"

She clenched Grandma Mobley's hand tighter. "If there are any others, we haven't been able to find signs of them. Besides, their most likely targets will be the two of us. We are the two most prominent and powerful in the coven. Without us, the whole thing falls apart."

"You don't have successors?"

"Of course we do. We chose Laverne and Candace for that honor." Lifting her chin as if to rise above her dark thoughts, she said, "Understand that until this all began, we had no idea that anybody other than the man himself knew what to do. Smashing the bricks, destroying them physically, does not harm us. It is saying the man's name while carving a special symbol that burns the spirit out of the clay."

A dread silence fell on the room. Max felt bad for the women, despite them being witches, and he wanted to help them — if for no other reason than to help Sandra. He knew this meant more to her than most cases. The witch connection touched a note in her that sustained long after it should have quieted down. But it was Sandra who broke the silence.

She walked over to Grandma Mobley and put out her hand. The old witch slowly shifted in her bed until her gnarled, broken fingers found Sandra's. Max watched an understanding look pass between them.

"We will find the bricks for you," Sandra said. "We will help as best we can."

Grandma Mobley's lips — thin flaps of wet skin — twisted into the approximation of a grin. Max wanted to throw up.

Chapter 17

WHEN MAX WOKE THE FOLLOWING MORNING, his muscles ached as if he had been throwing punches all night. He could not recall his dreams, but they hovered close enough to the edge of memory that he sensed they were dark and unpleasant. Despite the uneasy sensation, one look to his right dispelled all the darkness — Sandra slept next to him.

Careful not to wake her, he slipped out of bed and tiptoed downstairs to the kitchen. Max's mother had the boys under her personal house arrest, so he knew nobody would be knocking on their door that morning. Drummond might pop in — they hadn't seen him since Lena forced him into the Other — but that ghost would read the situation and get out.

In a few minutes, Max had coffee brewing, bacon cooking, bagels toasting, and eggs whisked up and ready to go. Humming an aimless tune, he set the table for two, poured a small glass of cranberry juice for each of them, and decided to place a candle on the table. Who cared if it was morning? Love never followed a timetable.

When he heard the toilet flush upstairs, he set the eggs in the pan. By the time Sandra thumped downstairs, Max had plated their breakfast and handed over a mug of coffee with a big grin and bright eyes. She took a sip, sat down, and frowned.

Not the reaction he had expected.

"What's the matter?" he said as softly as he could manage.

"We're not good right now. All of this — we're not at this stage yet."

"But I thought — I mean, I told you I'm behind you on all of this."

"That's not what you've been doing."

"I made a mistake. A lot of them. What else is new? But that doesn't mean —"

"Don't dismiss me like that."

"I'm not."

Between bites of bacon, she said, "Listen to yourself — Oh, what else is new? I make mistakes. You know me. But my heart's in the right place, so don't worry if I stomp all over your privacy and act as if I don't trust your judgment."

"That's not at all what I was saying, and you know it."

"Do I? Because not too long ago, you told me you were okay with me becoming a witch, and then suddenly we're back to the fear of what it'll do to me."

"I never agreed for you to *become* a witch. I agreed for you to study them, learn about them, research them."

"That's not how I remember it."

"Clearly."

Sandra chewed her bagel with more force than necessary. Max watched her aggressive display and couldn't figure out how this morning had gone off track so fast. Washing down her food with more coffee, she stabbed some eggs and followed that with a little more bacon.

At length, she said, "This isn't going to work if you continue to doubt me, if you won't trust me."

"I do trust —"

"Stop saying you do, when I can point to numerous times that you've done the exact opposite of trust. Trust is supposed to be the core of us. If we're to keep going forward, then we can't lose that."

Max's chest chilled. "We are not going to talk about what I think you want to talk about."

"I don't want to talk about it. I don't even want to think about it. But here's the hard truth — people change. We both are nothing like the naive couple who moved to the South with practically nothing to their name. Back then, you knew nothing of ghosts and witches and curses. None of this world existed for you. But now it does, and that has changed you. I've seen you become stronger, smarter, more passionate about your life. I've seen you develop the closest friendship I've ever known you to have."

"With Drummond?"

She let her fork fall to the plate. "So what if it's with a ghost? That just shows you how much this new life of ours has changed you. Have you ever given much thought to what it might have done to me? Or did you expect me to stay stagnant and never grow beyond the lovesick girl you first met?"

"Of course you're going to change. I know that."

"Then you've got to be open to those changes." She placed her hand atop his. Max wanted to see that as a positive sign, but her words did not match the sentiment. "Do you remember Christie Mund?"

"From Michigan? She was part of your Lady's Gang."

Many years back, after college, Sandra and four other women gathered for brunch once-a-month. A casual get-together meant to help keep their friendships alive. They called themselves the Lady's Gang.

"Christie had a tough job as social worker. Real heart-wrenching stuff. And every now and then, she'd unload some of it at our brunches. Listening to stories of abused and neglected children never made for a light morning, but we let her say what she needed to. You could see it in everything about her — that once she finished, her smile returned only brighter, her laughter returned but a little bit louder. By getting those stories out of her, she suddenly could face the world again." Sandra patted his hand. "Patience, hon, there is a point.

"See, her husband, Rex, never liked that she worked. I don't think you ever met him, but he was a Neanderthal with a brain forged in a rural backwater circa 1930. To him, women belonged in the home — possibly barefoot and pregnant — and men earned the money. It's worse than that really, but we don't need to go into it right now. Just know that he was an awful human being who saw his wife as his property.

"The only reason Christie worked was because he didn't earn enough money. Until he got promoted. Then he decided she needed to change. He put their marriage on the chopping block — either she do what he commanded or the marriage ended. So, she left her job. We saw her twice more and neither time did she look well. She had no more horrible stories to share but she did not smile or laugh or anything. And then she stopped coming at all.

"I don't know if she ever got the courage to leave him, but watching her I saw that no marriage can survive one spouse forcing the other to change in a specific way. The couple may technically stay married, but the love vanishes and it's replaced with resentment. I don't want to become Christie Mund. I don't want to resent you."

Max pulled his hand away. He hated to do it, but this conversation could not be smoothed over. "Your friend, and the many out there like her — they're not you. Christie didn't grow to resent her husband from that one instance. He clearly dominated her life, probably every aspect of her life, to the point that going out and fighting for other people's children gave her the bit of breathing room she needed. Being forced to quit that job may have sent her over the edge but her husband's behavior before that — it brought her to that edge. That's not you. You aren't stifled on all sides, controlled by dictatorial rule in the house, or anything like that. And if you feel that way, we need to have a much different conversation."

"I don't feel that way. That's not what I'm saying."

Max tapped the table. "I listened to you. Now, please, hear me out. You aren't being abused and nobody is trying to control your decisions. You know that. But you also don't get to make unilateral decisions that change the nature of our marriage, of our existence. We've both made that mistake before, and we shouldn't be doing it again."

"Damn, you absolutely refuse to see this for what is. You want me to listen to you? Listen to yourself. Every single time that you make a unilateral decision, you give your reason and apology and then that's it. I'm expected to accept it. But if I do it, I'm destroying us. That's the subtext between us way too often. Then you have the nerve to tell me it's all in my head. You fucking gaslight me with all this *nobody's trying to control you.*"

"That's not what I'm saying. I'm not trying to do anything

like that."

Sandra snapped out her napkin and wiped her mouth. "Here's what's going to happen. I'm going back upstairs. I'm taking a shower. And then, I'm going out to talk with the witches I know. I'll see what I can dig up on this man Grandma Mobley made her deal with, the book she used, and that kind of thing. I suggest while I'm getting ready, you go to the office and research whatever the hell you want to research. You want to help with this case? Great. Do that research. But I know you want nothing to do with this part of my life, so if you'd rather take on a cheating spouse case or something more mundane, be my guest."

"That's not fair."

"You're right about that. You haven't been fair to me about any of this."

"Honey —"

Sandra stood, her chair making a racket as she pushed back. "If you have any sense of what's good for you, you won't speak to me for a while."

As she marched upstairs, Max kept quiet. He cleared the dishes and replayed the last few minutes in his head. None of it made much sense to him.

Chapter 18

DRIVING TO THE OFFICE, Max's morning worsened when his phone rang and he saw *Mother* on the ID. Thankfully, that call went swiftly and with limited insult to his newly-formed parenting abilities — she only wanted to brag about how well things were going with the boys under her care. Max would happily endure her hubris if it meant getting a lid on that situation. Besides, she loved mothering PB and J even if it meant disciplining them — perhaps, especially when it meant disciplining them. Having been on the receiving end many times in his life, Max figured tomorrow the boys would be begging to go back to school.

As he entered his office, he cleared his mind of his mother and his wife so that he could focus on the case at hand. Despite Sandra's biting remarks, Max had no intention of bailing out. He would never leave her to fight alone. They were a team. No matter what.

While his laptop powered up, he pulled out his notebook and reviewed the little he knew. The second he could jump online and get to the search bar, he typed in the name he had been itching to research since the day before — George Black. The rest of the morning blurred by as he learned of this man's life and his work. Nothing could distract Max from his pursuit in research.

"I've been in front of you for three minutes. You ever going to look up?"

Nothing except that. Marshall Drummond floated a few feet from the desk like he had returned from a luxurious vacation.

"You okay?" Max asked. "Lena said she had sent you to the Other, so we weren't too worried, but still —"

"Don't get all choked up with your concern." Drummond

thrust his pale hands into his pockets and drifted toward the window. Gazing across the city, he said, "It didn't feel too good being thrown off like that. Not as bad as touching the solid world, but I wouldn't want to have to go through it again."

"Sorry. I didn't realize."

"It's okay. I've been hurt by witches before. Anyway, she did send me to the Other. I figured you'd be a while, so I made friends with Bernice, a dark-haired flapper killed by a mobster in 1927. At least, that's what she told me. We talked a bit but not too much. She worked a little magic on my bruises."

"Magic?"

"The kind that involves privacy and a lack of clothing."

"Someday, when my curiosity overcomes my revulsion, I'm going to have to get some details on how ghosts do that. Seems like you should pass through each other."

The corner of Drummond's mouth lifted. "Not at all. It's colder than you'd expect, but —"

"I don't want to know. I'm truly glad you're okay, so let's leave it at that."

"Fair enough." Turning back to the desk, he pointed to the notebook. "I know that look in your eye, and I see your scribbling, so out with it — what do you got?"

Unable to be coy about his work, he jumped to his feet, hooked the notebook in his arm and paced the office as he revealed his research. "George Black was one of those people every town has — a guy who lived an amazing life, did something incredible, and almost nobody knows who he is or anything about him."

Drummond flicked his hat back. "Gee, Professor, go ahead and enlighten me."

"Pay attention, there might be a quiz. George Black was born in 1879. His parents were former slaves, and after the war and emancipation, Black's father bought five acres of land in Randolph County. Get this — he bought it from his former master's plantation."

"I'm sure the ol' master cringed through that sale — lost the war and now he has to sell his land to the people he abused.

That's some sweet revenge."

"I doubt George's father saw it that way."

"True. No amount of revenge could ever make up for slavery, but it's still a nice image to have in my head."

"Anyway, they lived in a tiny cabin, and when I say *they*, I'm talking about the parents, their four boys, and one grandmother. It was a life you would expect for the time period — everybody working and not much time for education. Heck, even the grandmother did laundry for the white families and she lived to be a hundred and seventeen. George went to school long enough to learn the basics — the alphabet, some numbers, not much more though.

"In 1889, when George was ten, there was some trouble — or there wasn't. This is a fascinating guy because there's conflicting stories. One story says that George's half-brother had previously moved to Winston-Salem to make money in town, but instead, the boy started carousing with the wrong sort. So, George's father walked fifty miles to get the boy and stumbled into meeting a brickmaker who offered the father and son good work at a good price. The father moves the whole family to Winston-Salem, and though he died in 1890, the family stayed and the boys started working for the brickmaker. They hauled bricks from the mud mill — that's where the bricks are made from molds — and took them to pallets to dry. All day long. But other stories suggest that at ten years old, George, his father, and one brother walked to Winston-Salem because they heard they could make $1.50 per day working bricks together. And yet another story says he worked for the Hitchcock Brickyard where he went right into learning brickmaking."

"Either way the story ends up in the same place."

Max wagged his finger. "I don't agree. I mean, yes, the stories do technically end up at the same spot, but the motivation is different in each case."

"Is that important?"

"I don't know. I'm hoping you'll be able to hear something in all of this that I'm missing."

Drummond puffed up. "I'll do my best."

"However it went down, the whole family ended up living in Winston-Salem — eleven people by that point, all crammed into a one-room tenement. Fast forward to the 1920s. Black's been working the same for decades and all throughout those years, he's been learning his craft. He's also wondering why he has to struggle to live.

"The story goes that on one occasion, he said to his brother, 'They can pay us pretty good money, we do the work, and they make more money than we make. How come we can't make brick and get it all?' As luck would have it, his boss had an old, broken mud mill and gave it to Black to use for firewood. But George fixed that mill and started using it to make his own bricks.

"I don't know whether it was the care he put into his bricks, the molds he created, or something else, but George Black's bricks became the most desired bricks around. They were considered better quality and more durable than anybody else's. And when you consider how many bricks are needed to build a city —"

Drummond whistled. "That ain't no small thing."

"Another story about him says that sometime after Black had started his own brickmaking business, R. J. Reynolds rode out on horseback to visit. He ordered five hundred thousand bricks. After seeing the result, he came back and ordered a million more. I mean, that's a lot of bricks, but that isn't all of them. These bricks are all over Winston-Salem — mansions and homes, Old Salem is filled with them, especially the fire house, the Salem College Library, and tons of other places.

"Even after technology changed and the process became more and more automated, or at least, mechanized, Black insisted on doing it all by hand. Then things took another big turn in 1971. Charles Kuralt interviewed him for *The CBS Evening News*. This brought a small amount of fame to Black. People wanted to hear from him. He traveled to Guyana to teach villagers how to make bricks, he spoke to numerous groups, and even got invited to the White House. It was Nixon at the time, but still, that's pretty cool."

"And the old man was in his nineties at the time."

"That's right. He went on to be over a hundred. Amazing life. A really unique life."

"But?"

"I can't find anything that suggests he was involved with the occult, the supernatural, witchcraft, or any of it. I thought maybe he provided the bricks for one of the early homes of the Mobley Coven, but there's nothing. Not even a hint that he ever came into contact with them."

"Maybe he did without knowing."

"I thought about that. According to the coven, Eunice Mobley had her spirit bound to the North Carolina red clay and that's the key ingredient to his bricks."

"Also Candace's dying word was *Black*. So, it seems pretty clear."

Max wrinkled his face. "It's not enough. All we have are the stories people are telling us. The research isn't backing it up. In fact, the research isn't pointing to anything verifiable."

"When has that ever been an issue for you? I've seen you connect dots so far apart they might've been in different states. Where's your trusty intuition?"

"Maybe that's what's bothering me. It isn't kicking in. Something doesn't add up."

Drummond pursed his lips as he circulated through the room. While passing over Max's desk, he paused. "What's that list?"

"Addresses of buildings verified to have used George Black's bricks. There are quite a few still in existence."

"And you don't see the connection?"

"I haven't had a chance yet to really look at it."

"Third one from the top — the Latino Community Credit Union."

Max picked up the paper. "What about it?"

"It's located at 658 Waughtown Street."

"Isn't that where the pharmacy is?"

"Now it is. But a bunch of years ago, it was the credit

union."

Max pressed the paper against the desk, examining each address closely. His shoulders drooped. "I don't see the Science Center listed here."

"You wouldn't. That part of the building we were in was secret and old. Probably a remnant of a different building altogether."

Though he did not fill up with confidence, he saw no better avenue to follow. "Okay. I need some lunch, but afterwards, I'll get started researching these addresses. If Sandra will talk to me ever again, we can get her to call upon her real estate contacts for more details, if we need them."

Drummond snickered. "Sometimes, Max, you're a bit slow."

"Gee, thanks. That's all I need today — to be insulted by a ghost."

"You don't have to get Sandra's help and you don't have to sit at your computer for hours. For this, we need to do it the old fashioned way — honest detective work."

"And that means what?"

"We're hoofing it."

Chapter 19

THE IDEA OF BEING AN OLD SCHOOL DETECTIVE for an afternoon actually held some appeal. But after a short lunch and driving all over the city, walking around brick building after brick building, Max discovered that "old school detective" meant aching feet, a sweaty back, and no progress. For his partner, however, the day had been a thrilling nostalgia trip.

"I tell ya," Drummond said as Max drove to the last location on their list, "this is what the gig should never have gotten rid of. You spend so much of your time at a computer or in the library, but this is where the real work is. Getting into the grit of it all."

"What grit? We haven't found anything useful."

"Trust me. We've found more than we know. It's like your research — you read and read, and it seems like all of what you've learned is not really helpful. Then something happens and it all connects."

Max tagged his fingers as he counted off. "Former Wells Fargo bank, seven private homes on four different streets in three different neighborhoods — all very nice houses, the pharmacy, Old Salem, even the YWCA, and not a single place has had anything to help us."

"Maybe. Maybe not. They all had bricks made by George Black. That's got to be something."

"The man made millions upon millions of bricks in his lifetime. Finding a building with his bricks ain't that hard."

"That only makes it harder on us to find the right bricks. Come on, pull yourself together. This kind of pessimism doesn't look good on you."

"Yeah? Well, optimism is a weird look on you."

"Will you allow me to find a few enjoyable moments in a

case I wanted nothing to do with? Sheesh, I thought you'd like doing onsite research like this. Are you grouching because of your fight with Sandra?"

"Probably." Max turned onto 25th Street. "I wish I understood why she's pushing back so hard."

"You had PB follow her."

"I apologized for that. And I am sorry. I know it was stupid—"

"I told you that."

"— but I can't see why this is where the line in the sand is drawn. It's like I'm a friend saying that maybe you shouldn't keep looking down the barrel of that loaded gun, and she keeps replying that I'm a bad person for trying to stop her from shooting her head off."

Drummond rubbed his chin but said nothing.

"Really?" Max said. "Now is the time you're going to get all quiet on me?"

"I've heard enough of this argument over the last year or so that I know no matter what I say, you are determined to only see things from your side. Same with her. Normally, you two are good at fighting things out and getting on with it. I don't know why this one has you both stymied, but I'm not getting in the middle of it. Not more than I have to."

Turning onto North Patterson, Max stayed silent the rest of the drive. What more could he say? Drummond showed excellent judgment to keep out of it, and anything Max wanted to share, he really needed to share with Sandra.

He pulled in a small lot and shut off the engine. "Let's go take a look at another bunch of bricks." He had a strong feeling that he would be dreaming about red clay bricks all night long.

Standing before a building much like the pharmacy, Max had to assume they were designed around the same time, if not by the same architect. Like the pharmacy, this building had a narrow, elongated shape with a large chimney and an entirely brick exterior. The roof had been made of wood and painted white. This particular roof rose high at a steep angle.

As they headed toward the front, Max noticed how the

concrete sidewalk gave way to a brick walkway leading to the entrance. A sign to the side of the glass door read — *Black-Phillips-Smith Government Building.*

"Maybe we got it wrong," Drummond said. "Maybe Candace Mobley meant the Black that this building was named for."

"Doubtful. Too many pieces connected to George Black."

"But not all of them."

Max tried the door. Locked. "Figures. Any bright ideas?" Drummond opened his mouth, but Max added, "That don't involve breaking and entering?"

"I don't always suggest that. It just happens to be an effective method of finding information others don't want you to have."

"So that was going to be your suggestion?"

Drummond's offended glare brought a chuckle up Max's throat. "For your information and edification, I've got more than one trick up my sleeve. Now, in this case, I'm telling you that there's no reason to break into that building. We're not looking for anything on the inside."

Max paused. The ghost was right. "Let's keep looking."

As they turned the corner, they saw several things at once — none of which were good. First, they saw that a drive-thru overhang had been built and like the building, it had been built of bricks. Even as Max thought about the boring task of going over all those bricks, his mind processed the recessed corner in the back and the bald man with a flaming cross tattoo on his arm. The man locked eyes with Max before tearing off toward the back. Finally, right before Drummond yelled "He's a Goodman hunter!", Max noticed the brick in the bald man's hand.

Breaking into a sprint, Max pursued the man. They crossed a back street before Max noticed Drummond soaring by his side. The bald man dashed across a corner lawn and down a street of small homes with small yards. He shot up a driveway and into the back.

"Keep on him," Max said and Drummond followed the

man.

Max, however, kept to the street. He pushed himself harder with the hope of getting ahead of the man. As Max turned up the next street, he saw the man race into another yard with Drummond close behind.

Ignoring the pounding in his chest, Max called upon every bit of strength he had to push his legs faster. He darted ahead to the next street, saw that the man hadn't reached the yards yet, and smiled — right before a car pulled out in front of him.

His meager martial arts training saved him serious injury. Instead of smashing straight into the Toyota Prius, Max's new instincts reacted. He jumped forward, rolling across the hood and falling to the driveway on the other side.

"What the heck are you doin?" the driver yelled as she stepped from the car. Though only in her twenties, she acted hardened by a long, brutal life. "You think I got time to spend fixing dents from stupid kids playing around?"

Max rolled up to his feet, but it was over. Drummond rushed over to make sure he was okay. The Goodman hunter had escaped.

"I'm talking to you," the woman went on, ignoring the obvious mistake she had made. "You can't be running around here like that. Grown man like you. People live here. And look at that scratch. Who's going to pay for that?"

"Ma'am, I'm sorry."

"Don't *Ma'am* me. How old do you think I am?"

Drummond arrived, reached out, and placed his hand inside the woman's head. A short touch and she passed out from the cold. Drummond groaned. "Worth it," he said, rubbing his hand.

Together, the two walked back to the government building. At first, neither spoke. Max needed to catch his breath and stop sweating while Drummond needed to stop the throbbing pain in his hand. By the time they reached the section of the brick building where they had seen the Goodman hunter, both were ready to work.

About chest high, they saw the hole where the man had

dislodged the brick. Max looked over all the surrounding bricks as Drummond checked up at the roof height.

"I don't see anything suspicious other than the obvious," Drummond said.

"Yeah, me neither." Max inspected the hole. "Here's something."

Drummond dropped in close. "What do you got?"

"The brick he took — it wasn't one of George Black's. Look at the bricks all around it. Each one has a sharp edge, precision cut, and each one looks identical. Very little variation. That's done by a machine, not by hand. The ones from our knees down are Black's, and on both sides, too. But this small patch here came from somewhere else."

"You can tell that?"

"You can't? We've been looking at George Black's handmade bricks all day."

Drummond clapped his hands together and pointed at Max. "See that? Get into the grit of it all and you start to see things you would've missed sitting at your desk."

"Maybe." That was as much praise as Max dared give the ghost. He pulled out his phone and took several pictures of the wall. "For now, though, we're going back to the office. It's time to do research my way."

Two cars nearly collided on the street, and the long honk of one horn drew Max's attention. The second car involved screeched away from the scene. The first driver flipped off the escaping car, and then asked everyone standing around, "Did you see that? Anybody get his plates? Please? Anybody see the guy?"

Max did. But he wouldn't be helping the driver. Not when the man zipping off down the street was Leon Moore.

Chapter 20

BY THE TIME THEY RETURNED TO THE OFFICE, Max's stomach grumbled for an early dinner. No time to eat, though. He had research on his mind. That, and Leon Moore, but thoughts of Leon, Mother Hope, and the Magi only pushed him to research harder. Perhaps recognizing Max's need to focus, Drummond slid into his bookshelf and disappeared for a while. Max sat at his laptop and got to work.

Thankfully, he had a lot of details. For him, researching with so much information already known was like basic algebra. All the given numbers nearly provided the entire answer, and he merely had to solve for *x*. In this case, he had the bricks, the brick master, addresses, years — all he needed to find was who made the different bricks, the non-Black bricks.

In less than fifteen minutes, he had the answer. Another fifteen and he had more of the story coming to light. But he also had questions.

"Out with it already," Drummond said after being called back into the office.

Max poured a mug of coffee. "The brick that the Goodman hunter took came from Perklin Brickmakers. They're now defunct, but in the early-2000s, they were doing well. Unfortunately for them, they did so well that they diversified their excess cash into real estate. The crash in '08 wiped them out."

"I don't doubt you for a second, but you've got to satisfy my curiosity. How can you know where a single brick came from?"

"Because while George Black's bricks are known for their durability, they're not invincible. Things happen, and bricks need to be replaced. Perklin made a great brick, apparently, and they became the go-to people for buildings that originally had only Black's bricks. The government building we checked out had an incident in 1997. A drunken idiot smashed his truck into the side of the building taking out a chunk of the wall."

"And they called Perklin to repair it."

"Exactly."

Drummond lowered his head as he thought. "Hold on there. Are you saying the Goodman hunters made a mistake? They got the wrong brick?"

"They knew exactly what bricks to destroy twice before. This was not a mistake."

"But why take a Perklin brick? It's not got the right clay."

Max set his mug down and spread his hands on the desk. "Unless it does. We've assumed this whole time that Black's bricks were the ones that used the cursed red clay."

"Candace said the name Black. And Grandma Mobley's story also pointed to Black."

"All of which set us on the right course. But here's something else I found out — one of the reasons, possibly the main reason, that Perklin became the number one source for replacing Black's bricks was because the red clay they used specifically matched up with Black's. They had set aside a special clay for that purpose."

"You think that clay was the cursed clay. Sitting around in the ground all that time."

"It would explain something that's been bothering me from the start. If these witches knew about the bricks, why didn't they go get the bricks themselves a long time ago? Why wait until a crisis? But the truth is, they didn't know. All along, they thought Grandma Mobley's spirit was safely tucked in the ground. No matter what they've said to us, they had no idea about the bricks until this all started up."

Drummond's head bobbed up and down. "You've convinced me."

"The next question I've got is about these Goodman hunters. Why did they steal that brick? The others they destroyed, they used that symbol and fried the bricks which killed the witches. But this time, they cut out the brick. Why?"

The gentle voice of Max's wife came from the doorway. "That one's easy."

"Doll, it's good to see you." Drummond flew over and gave a short bow.

She grinned. "Sometimes, you can be a real goof." She sat behind her desk and kicked her feet up. "They need the witches to be present when they torch the bricks. It's not enough to simply say the name and draw the symbol. The spirit trapped in the brick must be present with the body to which it belongs. And the body must be purified in blessed water during a specific spell before sundown of the same day. The first time, at the pharmacy, was sort of like a drive-by. The second time, they managed to kidnap Candace and bring her to the brick. But the rest of the coven is on alert now. They're being cautious wherever they go, and doing what they can to shield Lena and Grandma Mobley specifically. The hunters are having a harder time getting hold of the witches they need."

Max said, "So they figured they might as well collect the bricks while they can."

"They can hold onto the bricks as long as it takes. After all, that was the whole point of the deal Eunice made — her spirit won't leave those bricks."

"Until they're destroyed."

"That's what the coven told us, but you can't believe everything they say. Maybe Grandma Mobley is cursed to suffer even after her death."

Max tried to blot out that horrible idea. He still had hope that his own curse could be removed at some point. But if a witch as powerful as Grandma Mobley — not just her but her entire coven — if they couldn't free her from a curse, then perhaps he should rethink the possibilities of his future. No matter how ugly.

"I'm liking everything I hear," Drummond said. "Let's say we've got this right — my gut says we do — then we've got a few avenues available to us. We could circle the wagons around the coven or even just Lena and Grandma Mobley. Do everything we can to protect them which would essentially create a stalemate."

"That won't work. It's only good short term." Sandra rose from her chair, taking control of the room as if she stood taller than Drummond. "Both sides are willing and able to take on something like this for decades. While you've got a few centuries ahead of you, Max and I won't live that long. And I'm sorry if this disappoints you, but I have no intention of sticking around here as a ghost just to go on protecting a witch coven from a bunch of idiots."

"I'd love for you to stick around with me, but I don't expect it. I'm just savoring the time I have with a looker like you."

"Aren't you the rascal?"

Max cleared his throat. "Quit egging him on."

Drummond thrust out his hands. "I like being egged on."

"What other choice do we have? I mean about the bricks."

"The way I see it, if we don't protect the witches, we're left with two viable options. Either we come up with some way to take out the Goodman hunters —"

"That ain't happening," Max said. "We're not killers."

"Then we get the last brick ourselves."

Max paused, letting that idea sink in. Getting the brick would stop the Goodman hunters from killing another woman with this horrible curse, but it would not protect them from other forms of attack. There would also be a new problem — the hunters might come after the brick, and since Max had no intention of letting the witches have the brick, that meant the hunters would be coming after him, Drummond, and Sandra. But those were problems to be dealt with once they had the brick. If they didn't get hold of it, no speculation mattered. That still left one crucial hurdle.

"How do we find it?"

"We have the addresses. We know where all the bricks are. Why don't we just go look?"

"I think death is making you a bit crazy. There are millions of bricks out there that Black made. And while only a small percentage had to be replaced with Perklin bricks, it's still a huge number. Say it's as low as one percent. One percent of a million is ten thousand. And there are way more than one million. Might even be tens of millions. We could have over a hundred thousand replacement bricks to have to go through."

"Even if you could do that," Sandra said, "it still won't work." She paused, and Max's stomach gurgled. He knew he wouldn't like what she said next. "Even if you could isolate every last Perklin brick and lined them all up next to each other, you'd never be able to tell which ones held Grandma Mobley's spirit and which ones were just bricks. It's not like they glow orange or have a big arrow pointing at them."

Wishing back the words in his throat but knowing he had to move forward, he asked, "What do we do then? How do we find a specific brick amongst all of them?"

"You know how."

Drummond's face screwed up as he took off his hat. "Well, I don't know how. Why don't one of you tell me? You can't tell by looking, there aren't any marks. I suppose since a witch was involved at the beginning of all of this, we might need to cast a ... oh." The ghost eyed Max's tense glare then looked over at Sandra's stronger glower. "I think I'll go check on my 1920s gal in the Other. Give you some time to work this out." Not waiting for a reply, Drummond vanished.

A hundred thoughts raced through Max's head. He wanted to stop her from going any further with this impending argument, but he also wanted to finish it — get it done with and out of the way. He wanted her to finally listen to reason, but he also knew they needed to find that brick.

"There," she said, pounding her hand against her desk. "You're fighting it out in your head, and that is exactly the problem. If you truly wanted me to stop with witchcraft, there would be no debate in your head. You should be screaming at me, yelling at the top of your lungs how wrong I am to keep pushing. But you don't."

"You're my wife, not my property."

"Oh, don't even — the only reason you hesitate is because you need me to cast a spell to locate that brick. That's it. You're no better than those Goodman hunters. They decry witchcraft and magic, and they go around killing suspected witches, but how do you think they found the bricks? Same way. They cast a spell. For crying out loud, look at how they destroy the bricks — with a symbol, a word, purified water, and a recitation. That's a spell. That's witchcraft. They're hypocrites, and so are you."

"That's not fair. I'm not going around trying to kill you. I'm fighting you on this to save you."

"Do you have any clue how condescending you sound?"

"Huh? What did I do now?"

"This entire time you have stood in my way claiming you're trying to protect me, to save me from the evils of witchcraft. But did it ever once occur to you that I can handle myself? Did you ever think that maybe I'm strong enough and smart enough to investigate witchcraft without becoming an evil creature that you'd have to fight someday?"

Max trudged across the office, bringing his face close in on her. "Why the heck are you determined to twist everything I'm saying into something malicious? I'm your husband. I love you. I'm not trying to undercut your ability or bash down your equality or anything like that — and you damn well know it. We're married, and that means we look out for each other, we protect each other, and if necessary, we save each other — even when our spouse can handle it alone."

Sandra put her hands on her hips and stepped so close that her nose brushed against his. "That sounds so noble and good. Except you're lying. If what you said was true, you wouldn't keep asking me to perform spells. If you honestly wanted to protect me from witchcraft, you'd find another way to solve our problems. You would have rather let the case fail, deal with the consequences of an angry coven, than watch me cast another bit of magic."

Max whirled away, plopped onto the couch with his arms crossed, and scowled. "Fine, then. Don't cast a spell to find the brick."

"Now you're just saying that because I made my point."

Slapping his arms at his sides, Max uttered a frustrated cry.

"Unbelievable. No matter what I say, you'll make it wrong."

"Because in all of this time, over the last few years that this fight keeps coming back up, you've yet to be one hundred percent honest with me." She placed herself at the other end of the couch. In a softer voice, she said, "Please, hon. Talk with me."

"What do you want me to say?"

"The truth. You're not mad at me for learning about witches or witchcraft. You're not mad at me for casting spells. Is it that I see all ghosts, that I knew about this world my whole life? Do you think I brought all of this chaos onto us?"

Max turned towards her. "No, honey, not at all. I don't blame you for anything. And I don't regret moving down here and learning about ghosts and everything. Strangely enough, our lives have become better for it."

"Then what?"

"I have never doubted you. Know that deep in your heart. I am by your side. Always. But that doesn't mean I don't have fears. And it's not that I think you'll be seduced by the power of witchcraft and turned into a version of Mother Hope or Grandma Mobley. That's not it at all."

But Sandra pulled away. "You've said all of this before. Nothing's changing, and I'm telling you we can't keep on like this. It'll ruin everything."

Max put out his hand. "Stop guessing what I'm going to say and please listen. You don't want our marriage ruined — well, neither do I. I'm trying to tell you what's going on."

Though she did not shift towards him, he could see the change in her demeanor. The fire had dimmed. "I'm listening," she said, and he believed it.

With his mouth dry and his nerves jangling hard, he inhaled sharply. "When we were in college, shortly before I met you, I had a friend — Ted. Good guy, smart, a real math whiz. If things had gone different, he probably would have some lucrative job in Silicon Valley. But, the last I heard of him, he was a heroin addict, shooting up in alleyways and wasting away. I've seen addictive behavior and what I see in a lot of witches is the same thing."

"But I'm not —"

"Let me speak, please. I know you're not like that. I've known you a long time. You've never fallen into ruts of behavior. You don't have an addictive personality. But just because you're not a drug addict, doesn't mean you should be hanging out with drug addicts. Plus, the fact that you can handle a low level of witchcraft with such ease means you're likely to think you can handle the heavier stuff as well, and there's no proof of that. You've already done some serious spells that I wish you never had to do. We've been lucky with that, but why keep rolling the dice when you're ahead?"

Max grabbed the top of his head and closed his eyes. None of this had come out right. And he could feel the pressure in the room rising. If he didn't get through to her, if he didn't mine out the truth from himself, she would end up right about it all. Their marriage would be in trouble. Not at first. Maybe not for years. But this fear in him had already burrowed into the foundation of their marriage — their trust. It was a monster in larval form, growing stronger while eating away at the pillars of their union. If left unchecked, eventually it would take over, their marriage would end, and Max would be left wondering what had happened.

"I'd be helpless to stop it."

"Stop what?" Sandra said.

Max reached out for her shoulder but held back. "All of it. Everything. We've always solved our problems — not just ones between us, but cases and dangers and everything — we've always succeeded by barreling through. We're like surfers staying right on the edge of the wave. Even before North Carolina, before Drummond and all of it, that's the way we lived. That's the way we manage to have some control over our lives. We get in front of a situation, head it off, redirect it to suit our goals or needs or wants.

"But this is different. You want to go down a rabbit hole where I can't follow you. If you end up in trouble, I won't be able to help. Not on my own. I mean look at this coven. If that were you, if you ended up with your soul spread throughout the clay of the entire state, I wouldn't have the power to fix that. Either I'd have to let you suffer or I'd be forced to go to a witch like Mother Hope. And you know that a witch is going to make me pay dearly to get her help.

"It's not even that, though. Forget that example." He scratched his head. "It's more basic. I'm, well, I guess I'm helpless here. I can't force you to stop and I can't do anything to barrel through. All I'm left with is to stand at the side and watch." Tears dribbled down his cheeks. "Do you get what I'm saying? If things go badly, if you succumb to the dark evilness that it seems most witches fall prey to, I'll be helpless to do anything but watch the woman I love disappear before my eyes. That's not right. It's not fair. And that's what this is all about."

There. He had done it. The truth. He bent his head towards his knees as a sob heaved from his chest. He couldn't hold it back as he kept picturing Sandra wasting away like Grandma Mobley. He could feel her eyes upon him, and he wanted nothing more than to escape the office and her response.

Sandra placed her hand on his back. He shuddered as he held in another sob. "Now, I understand," she said.

A minute passed before he straightened. He grabbed a tissue, blew his nose, and regained his composure.

She kissed his cheek. "No matter what happens to me, you have something nobody else does — my heart. That's not just sweet words. My undying love is for you, and that means that should your fears come true, and I somehow fall into the world of dark magic, you are connected to me through our love. Nobody else will be able to reach me. You will be my lifeline, my rope back to sanity. You're not helpless at all. You're the strongest force to saving me."

Red-eyed and sniffling, he said, "Which means that, despite all I have to say, you're still going ahead with it all, with witchcraft."

"You keep missing the point. You have my heart, and I have yours. You fear witchcraft and its power, and that's good. We both should fear it. But you have to do something far more important than fear. You have to trust me. Me. Your wife. Your love. Trust me. Trust that I know my strengths and weaknesses. Trust that I understand how far I can go with something. Trust that I love you so much, I will never put that in jeopardy, because more than any power witchcraft could bring me, I want to always come home to your love."

The office phone rang startling both Max and Sandra. They smiled as Sandra answered the phone.

"Hello, Porter Agency," she said, and Max could tell by her expression that his mother had called. "No, he's not here. What? You were supposed to ... fine, fine. We're on it." She hung up and faced Max. "Your mother and PB had a bit of shouting match over his going back to school tomorrow. He stormed out. That was five hours ago and he hasn't returned or called or anything."

Chapter 21

LIKE MANY FAMILY EMERGENCIES that occur all over the world, this one mixed heart-pounding worry with sense-dulling boredom. Max and Sandra raced over to Mrs. Porter's apartment, their fears for PB pulsing through their veins like a thrash metal band in full rage. Before they had left, Drummond volunteered to scour the city streets for the boy but that did nothing to calm their frayed nerves. Once they reached the apartment, once they saw that Jammer J had stayed back and was safe, once they heard the story from Mrs. Porter, they had little else to do but sit and wait.

The police would not be of any help. Too early to call in a missing person, for one. But also, Max did not want to risk sending PB into Social Services. No *risk* about it — if they found out that PB's unofficial guardians drove him to run away, it would be over for the Porters. PB would be taken away and Social Services would probably take J, too.

"We should go out and look for him," Mrs. Porter said. "Why aren't we doing anything?"

Sitting with her on a couch, Max held her by the shoulder. "I've got my best man on the job. If he can't find PB, then PB's left the city."

An hour later, as night descended on them, Drummond arrived. "I found him."

Max did not look up. His mother had seen him talk with Drummond before, but it only convinced her that her son had a possible mental illness. Lifting a hand behind Mrs. Porter, Max gave Drummond a thumbs-up.

"Honey," Sandra said with forced lightness. "You should go check on your man. I'm sure we could all use an update."

"Sure. I'll be back soon."

Drummond waited to appear again until Max had entered the elevator. "The kid's okay."

Max wanted to hug the ghost for starting right off with the most important news. He texted Sandra, told her that PB was fine, but asked that she not tell his mother — not until he had a chance to talk with PB. Sandra reluctantly agreed to do as he wished, finishing her text with three words that hit home: *I trust you.*

"Where is he?" Max asked as he left the building and headed towards his car.

Drummond said, "His old home. I didn't think to look there at first because, frankly, of all the places that kid could go, why would he return to one of the most miserable of his life?"

"He doesn't have a loved one to go running to for comfort, and that place is about the only thing he ever could have called his own. He found it. He defended it. He survived because of it."

"If you say so. Still seems nutty to me. But he's there, so who am I to say otherwise? You want me to come along with you?"

"I can handle this. And I need you to do something else."

"Back on the case?"

"Yeah. I want to find the clay deposit Perklin Bricks used back when they were making replacements for the Black bricks."

"Does this mean we're going to be casting a spell?"

"I'm not happy about it, but I don't see another option — not if we want to save Lena and Grandma Mobley."

Drummond stopped at Max's car. "Do we? I mean this coven has been around a long time. Chances are they've done some bad things."

"First, we're not going to sit by and let these women die — witch or no witch. Second, do you really want to explain to Sandra any of what you just said?"

"Partner, you make excellent points. I'll go find the clay deposit."

After Drummond left, Max drove back to the office. He

walked to the corner coffee shop. They were cleaning up to close, but they still sold him the last two bagels and two bottles of water. Then he headed a block over to the section of demolished buildings and overgrown lots.

This was the place Max had first known PB — a boy, living on the streets, taking shelter between a makeshift lean-to and the remains of a brick wall. He would visit regularly, always bringing a little food and some water in the mornings. Until one day, when Max offered PB a job.

As Drummond had indicated, Max found PB sitting against the wall where his old home had once been. As he approached PB, he raised the bag of bagels and smiled.

PB took one bagel and a bottle of water. "I figured you'd show up eventually. You're not too good at letting people do what they want when you don't agree with them."

Max frowned. "I don't know how take that."

"Not my problem."

After sweeping aside some rocks and pebbles, Max sat on a flat piece of concrete. He opened his water bottle and swigged back a few gulps. Though he wanted to look directly into PB's eyes and set the boy straight, he knew he'd get more out of showing patience — especially after noting the tearstains glinting on the boy's cheeks under the moonlight.

A minute went by without a word. Then PB drank some water and nibbled on his bagel. Rolling a pinch of bagel between his fingers, he said, "I'm sorry about yelling at your mom. I didn't mean to fight with her."

"I know. She knows, too."

"I ain't changing my mind, though. That school is for other people. Not me. It's full of rich kids and kids with parents. Even the poor kids got at least one. They look down on me. I can tell. I'm good at reading people, you know that, and I could see how they all thought of me — slow, stupid, ugly."

"None of that's true."

"I didn't say I believed them. Fuck them. I'm the best thing that school ever saw. They were lucky to have me for a day. I'm just saying all that nasty crap is the way they saw me. You all put me in with a bunch of pricks. I'm being honest here."

"You never really tried to make it succeed, though. Since we're being honest."

"What good would it do? We both know I don't know what they know."

"You're a smart kid."

"But I ain't had the books they had. I didn't get the advance mathematics or whatever they call it. They're going to ask me questions I can't answer. It's like when people talk to somebody with a stutter — they assume the guy's an idiot just because it takes him longer to get the words out. But everything's fine inside his head, it only seems like he's slow."

Max dug his heel at the dirt beneath him to keep from gazing at PB. "I'm not sure what to say. In case you missed it, I'm new to the parent thing. Not that I'm trying to be your daddy or anything, but you know what the deal is. If we don't start acting like your parents, your guardians, then the state will take you away."

"Not if I'm not there."

"Right. And I guess you'll be taking Jammer J with you, too. Otherwise, the state will take him."

"Me and him were fine a long time before you showed up. We can do it again."

"Except he likes school."

PB hesitated. "I know."

Max's gut told him the time had come. He raised his head, and keeping the rest of his body still, he looked over at PB. "What's really bothering you? I know school can be intimidating, and I'm sure there are plenty of jerks you have to deal with."

"You're right on that." PB chuckled.

"But I also know that you and J both care a lot for my mother. I find it hard to believe that you were willing to yell at her and run off leaving her frantic with worry all because you didn't want to go back to school. And, unless I'm completely wrong, I'm pretty sure you like working for me. So this whole idea that you want to leave the Porter Agency, leave my mother, and leave J, that you want to walk away from everything and everyone you care about just to avoid going to school — well, that sounds a bit ridiculous to me. Something else is going on here."

PB shrugged and took another bite of his bagel.

"I can't force you to talk with me," Max said, "but I can promise you this — being honest about how you feel, what you thought, all of it, that's going to get you a lot further than shutting down. Come on. You've already turned away from all of us, so you got nothing to lose. Tell me what's going on, the full truth, and maybe I can help."

PB wriggled as his face contorted as if the words fought to exit his body. "I don't *want* to leave any of you."

"Then don't."

"But it's all going to change."

"Sorry to tell you this, but change is the only constant thing in life. Nothing stays the same forever. Why do you think school is going to change everything? Make it bad?"

PB turned sharply to face Max. "Because I'm going to fail. I can barely understand half the stuff they're talking about. I'm not smart enough, and they won't send me down to be with the little kids — they don't want those squirts to be intimidated by me. So I'm going to fail at everything there, and then either they throw me out or I drop out when I can. Then what? You really going to keep a piece of trash like me hanging around your office? Great. Then I'll be your little sympathy project. Each morning you can pat me on the head and find jobs for me that don't require too much thinking, but in the end, I'm going to read it on your face and Sandra's too — pity. I'm going to fail you both."

"And your solution is to run off and hide?"

"I don't have a solution!" PB's face reddened — not with embarrassment but rather from the effort to hold back his tears. "I came here to think."

Max wanted to lean over and hug the boy, but he kept still. The two listened to the city traffic and thought. When the answer hit Max, he wanted to both laugh and cringe.

"I've got one way to fix your problem."

PB threw a rock at a crumpled beer can. "I told you I'm not going back to that school."

"I heard you."

"J can go if he wants, that's his business, but I ain't going."

"Got it."

"And if I have to listen to —"

"Do you want to know my solution or not?"

PB paused, and Max worried the boy might run off again. Instead, PB cleaned his dirty hands across his jeans. "Go ahead already."

"Let's start with the most important thing — you have to trust me. Trust Sandra, too. We're not the enemy, and we care about you. Trust us. Trust that we're not mean, evil, spiteful people. That even if you do something we don't like, we've still got your back. That we're not going to abandon you or mistreat you or do anything harmful to you. I know we're not your parents, but we love you like you were our son."

PB grew redder and his chin trembled.

"If you're willing to trust us, then I think I know what we can do. You won't have to go back to that school again. We'll figure it all out. Together."

A tear escaped his clamped emotions and rushed down his face. PB wiped it away like swatting aside a pestering fly. Finally, he nodded.

"Great." Max stood and offered his hand. "In the meantime, I've got a job for you."

PB jumped to his feet. He shook Max's hand, sniffled, and said, "You got it, Bossman. You know I can do anything for the team."

"I hope so. Because Sandra can't know what you're up to. You good with that?"

"I have to be, right? I have to trust you."

"Yeah," Max said, trying not to think of the argument with his wife.

Chapter 22

"I'M GLAD YOU GOT HIM BACK," Sandra said, "but how exactly are we keeping him out of school?"

"One problem at a time, hon."

The sun had gone down hours ago, and Max drove through the dark streets heading out of Winston-Salem towards the old Perklin clay deposit. Though the building no longer housed an active company, somebody still retained ownership and liability. When Max pulled up to the curb a block away from the entrance, he found exactly what he had expected — a derelict brick building surrounded by chainlink fencing and one, lone guard stuck on the graveyard shift. Darkness engulfed the grounds and only two bulbs stuck high on wooden posts lit the area.

"This is the place," Drummond said from the backseat. "You ready, doll?"

Sandra patted her coat pocket. Inside that pocket, she carried a small, leather bound notebook where she kept detailed information and instructions on the various spells she had learned about. Max tried not to think about that book.

She unlocked her seatbelt and turned to him. "You sure you're okay with this?"

"No choice, really," Max said. Before she could run with that comment, he added, "I'll do my part, don't worry. Just be quick."

Sandra and Drummond exited the car. Max gave them thirty seconds before driving into the empty parking lot. The guard watched intently as Max pulled into a space several feet further over than necessary — probably thrilled to have something actually happening for a change. Max got out of the car and made a show of pulling out his camera and affixing the right lens and flash onto it.

The guard approached — a little caution in his voice. "Can I help you?"

"You certainly can," Max said, putting as much energetic joy into his tone as he could muster. "My name's Frank Venice. I'm a reporter for Historical Carolinas — we're a small outfit that tries to preserve the great history of our great state. Anyway, have you ever heard of George Black?"

"You're a reporter?"

"Yeah, come here, I'll show all about it." Max opened his notebook on the hood of his car and waved the guard closer. As he pointed to his notes and explained the long history of George Black and bricks, the guard leaned over to read Max's handwriting. All the while, the guard had his back to his post. Drummond passed through the fence and quietly opened it to admit Sandra inside.

Rubbing the pain from his hand after he closed the fence, he saluted towards Max and the two scurried over to a clay hill that would never be utilized by Perklin Bricks again. The guard stepped back, but Max hurried to turn the page and show newspaper clippings depicting Black, his home, and his entire brick making operation.

The guard hiked up his pants. "That's all real interesting, but it don't explain what you're doing here so late at night."

Max opened a broad grin and chuckled. "Of course not. I apologize. I get excited about my work and forget all about the point. Journalism can do that. You ever do any reporting?"

Over the guard's shoulder, Max could see little of what went on inside the fenced area. But Drummond held still in the air, his pale light unable to illuminate his surroundings but standing out like a lighthouse in the fog. Sandra appeared to be crouching at the base of the clay mound with her book out and a flashlight in hand.

"Look, mister, you gotta go. Nobody's allowed here."

"Oh, but I forgot to tell you the whole point of why I'm here. See, Perklin Bricks is connected to this great man. It's really something. Let me show you."

Blue light flashed up from the clay like a camera taking a candid shot of Sandra and Drummond. The light bounced off every leaf and branch of the trees lining the parking lot. Raising his head toward the sky, the guard scrunched his brow.

Max said, "Must be heat lightning."

"Weatherman said nothing about storms."

"Come on over. Let me show the rest. I mean, I hope this isn't boring you. I can leave you alone if you really want, but I don't usually get to show people all the cool stuff I find."

"Don't people read your articles?"

Thanks to plenty of practice, Max had no trouble playing the role he set up. "Sure. But those are edited heavily. They've got to fill a small space and leave plenty of room for advertising."

"Ads — the scourge of the world."

"Amen, my friend."

The guard glanced at his watch. "I still have a few hours left to my shift. Sure, go ahead and tell me the rest."

Max took his time laying out the story of brickwork in Winston-Salem. Whenever he sensed the guard losing interest, he pointed to another part of the notebook or raised his voice with enthusiasm, but eventually, the story petered out.

Stretching his back, the guard said, "That's all kind of cool, I guess. But I gotta get back to my post."

"Of course," Max said. He glanced at the gate. Sandra and Drummond were walking toward it. "Um, before you go, can I at least get a picture of you?"

"Me?"

"For the article — I can use the perspective of a man who still guards the bones of the old Perklin shop. It'll be in the article, so you can show it off to your friends and family."

"Really? That'd be nice. Sure. Where should I stand?"

"Right there," Max said, pointing to a spot a few feet away. He made a mockery of photography by pressing buttons on his camera and turning the lens back and forth when he had only ever used the autofocus setting. Through the camera, he watched as Sandra slipped out, Drummond endured the pain of closing up the fence, and the two dashed off into the woods.

He snapped off several shots. "Great. Thank you for taking a little time with me."

"No problem," the guard said, gleeful and a bit proud. "We don't get much in the way of visitors out here, so we appreciate the chance to show what we do. And that stuff about George Black, that's cool stuff. I'll have to look into him."

After a few more pleasantries, Max packed up his work and drove off. Around the block, he found Sandra and Drummond waiting for him under the amber glow of a streetlight. They climbed in and off he drove.

"Well?" he asked.

"I'm fine, by the way," Sandra said.

Drummond leaned forward. "If you two start bickering again, I'm going to freeze both your brains. Get along now, fight it out elsewhere, or bottle it all up and get therapy for a few years, but stop it. I'm sick of working for this coven, so I need you both to be thinking and working at top level. The faster that happens, the faster I can be done with this case and go back to my lady in the Other."

Both Max and Sandra stared ahead as he drove the quiet streets. When they stopped at a light, its deep red bathing Sandra in angrier tones, she said, "I've got an address."

"You have a spell that gives out addresses?" Max said.

"No. It made a mark on a map that I had in my notebook. When we get back to the office, we can look it up on my laptop. But for now, we know it's in Thomasville."

"That's great. We're one step closer." As the light changed, he viewed her from the corner of his eye. Her mouth turned down and her eyes had narrowed. "What's the matter?"

"Don't get all worked up, but I felt something strange when I cast that spell."

Drummond said, "She's not talking about strange like witchcraft taking over her mind."

"Oh, right. I'm fine. The spell went off without a problem and I barely felt the magic going through me."

"*Through* you?" Max said.

"You didn't think it just appeared because I said some

words, did you?"

"I never gave it much thought. You can actually feel it happening? Feel yourself creating it?"

"Sometimes. But this spell is nothing big. Like I said, I didn't really feel it."

"But you felt something strange."

"I thought it was whatever remained of Grandma Mobley's spirit still shifting around in the clay. But that doesn't seem right."

Max glanced back at Drummond for a hint, but the ghost kept his head facing the window. "Are you saying it wasn't her? That maybe it was this evil man she bargained with?"

"I thought about that, too. Except based on what Lena described to us, that man had a tremendous amount of power. This felt too faint and not dark enough, not evil enough to be him. I don't know yet. Maybe I'm imagining things. Maybe the intensity of what we just did got me overly sensitive at that moment."

Max's stomach twisted. "Or maybe you actually touched part of this evil magic."

"Calm down, hon. Don't jump to the worst possibility yet. Please. Let me think this through. Trust me, remember? I know what I felt — it seemed familiar — all I need is a little time to figure out where I remember this from."

Despite wanting to pull the car over and scream at the night sky, Max nodded. "Okay. You think on it. I'll go look up the Thomasville address."

"It's late, hon. Let's go home. Sleep on it all. We'll figure it out in the morning when we're refreshed."

Max turned onto Silas Creek Parkway to head to their development. He glanced in the rearview mirror to suggest Drummond call it a night, too, but the ghost had already left. Probably headed to the Other and Miss 1920s. The corner of Max's mouth rose.

Chapter 23

MORNING ARRIVED FASTER THAN MAX HAD WANTED. After they returned the night before, Sandra went straight to bed, but Max stayed up in his study. He made short work of locating the Thomasville address — an empty warehouse from the furniture heyday. Two big problems faced them — the building was entirely made of brick and it was situated a few blocks from the center of town. Not exactly the most inconspicuous place to be searching for a brick with a witch's spirit.

He spent another hour looking into the building's history but found nothing that jumped out as important to their case. Then he thought he'd watch a few music videos before turning in, but one link led to another and before he realized it, two hours had gone by. Worse — no matter how much nonsense he watched, he could not clear his head of the worry ping-ponging around his skull.

Sandra. Trusting her was easy. If she said she could handle the magic, he believed her. At least, he would work on it. But then she told him that she's sensing things — evil things. And he trusted that she did feel those things. That's the part that frightened him now. Worst of all — he knew they had to keep pushing.

But that didn't make it any easier to swallow.

"Morning," Sandra said.

Max jolted awake with a slip of paper stuck to his cheek. He couldn't recall falling asleep and felt even less rested. Smelling the musky odor rising from his body, he figured he should grab a shower before they headed off to Thomasville.

As he stood, Sandra said, "Your mother called."

He sat back down. "What's this morning's crisis?"

"J's back to school today. Apparently, he said he felt bad

that he liked it so much."

"I don't think I want to know how she handled that one."

A bagel popped up from the toaster. Sandra dug it out and buttered it. "I actually think she did a decent job. She and J seemed to have bonded well. She's like a kind Granny to him. Anyway, she said they had a good chat and that he went back happy and raring to do well."

"You believe that?"

"Better than the alternative."

"Speaking of which — what about PB?"

Sandra lifted her head. "He said you had a job for him. That's why your mother called. Was he lying? Did he run away again?"

"No, no. He's not lying. I'm a little foggy this morning. I'll take care of it."

"We've got to find a school for him."

"I'm working on it. But today, he's got some errands to run for me."

"What kind of errands?"

Drummond saved Max from further interrogation when he popped his head through the floor. "Good morning, you two. Are we all sorted out and ready to be the Porter Agency in top form today?"

"I've got to clean up. Then I'll be ready." Max walked off to the shelter of a shower.

Standing under the cascade of hot water, he had a brief reprieve from the current stresses. More than relaxation, however, he gained a little time to think. Because more than anything else in this case, time to think had been lacking. Even with the late nights available to him, too much pressure and too much fighting made deep thinking difficult. More often than not, he discovered that hours had gone by and his mind had piled up a muddled mess of facts and opinions that refused to connect. All of it centering on the one question — *Why?*

Drummond's charming voice cut into his thoughts. "You going to prune yourself in there or are we going?"

Covering his body like a teenager caught in the gym

showers, Max said, "We've talked about this. Don't be going through the walls into the bathroom."

"For Pete's sake, I'm in your bedroom. Well, most of me is. Only my head is in the bathroom, and I've got my eyes closed. Now, get a move on."

Max yanked a towel free from the rack and dried off. He tried not to think about why Sandra sent Drummond to get him instead of coming up herself. He knew the reason. They were on the road to mending after their fight, but nothing had been settled completely yet. Soon, though. He had a plan for that.

By the time he dressed and made it downstairs, Sandra opened the front door to usher him straight out. Once on the road, she opened her purse and dug out her book of spells.

"By the way, your mother called again. I am to inform you that using PB whenever it suits our business purposes is not going to enforce the idea that school is important. Also, you and I suck as parents. I'm paraphrasing."

Max got off Route 40 and took 109 toward Thomasville. "I'm not going to worry about her, PB, or J right now. Today, my focus is on this case. Like Drummond said — we're going to be the best version of the Porter Agency we can be. We do that, and we'll finish this case."

"That's right," Drummond said from the backseat. "I'm glad you're finally listening to me. Better late than never, and next time a witch coven wants to hire us, you remember that I'm the better judge on these things. Reminds me of when I was alive. I had this friend —"

Sandra said, "I need to prepare, go over this spell some more in my head. So let's keep the chitchat down, okay?"

"Anything you say, doll." Drummond pulled his Fedora over his eyes and leaned back.

Twenty minutes later, they hit the center of town. Two railroad tracks ran straight through the middle with roads paralleling the tracks creating a center causeway. Several blocks to the right, the old train station remained, and directly in the middle, a giant upholstered chair stood — both a symbol of the town's former glory as a prominent furniture supplier to the world and as a reminder that Thomasville was also connected to the title Chair City.

The design of the storefronts lining the roads could have been pulled out of any Norman Rockwell painting. And most of them were brick. But as Max drove over the railroad tracks and made a left, he saw their destination and nothing felt very Norman Rockwell. In fact, despite the bright morning or the traffic or the people walking their dogs, seeing that long, rectangular brick building filled Max with dark dread.

Without a word, Sandra looked up from her book and spied the building, too. Max could feel her tense up. Her breath caught in her throat. This was definitely the place.

Further on, across the street from the building, Max parked in a small lot. They walked over to the warehouse and toured the perimeter — mostly to get their bearings but also to build a little courage. Drummond followed them, unwilling to cut inside without them.

"It's not just me, then," Max said. "This place feels different."

Sandra nodded as she gazed up the steep brick wall. "There's something very unsettled here."

"Ghosts?"

Sandra pointed to the empty doorway, a few empty windows, and as they turned the corner, several spots by the walls. "Plenty."

"Don't ask," Drummond said. "I ain't going to chat with any of them. They don't look right in the head. And some of them are kids. Kid ghosts are creepy."

"That feeling I had last night at the Perklin clay deposit — well, I've got it a lot worse here."

Max frowned. "You said that it was a familiar feeling."

"I was wrong. Not familiar. Just dark."

Drummond said, "Dark, creepy, unsettling — I think we're all clear on how much we don't like this place."

Max held back his tongue. He didn't feel much like bantering anyway. "Let's get this over with. I don't want to hang out here any longer than we have to."

"You got that right."

Sandra stopped near a window under which a mass of weeds grew tall. "I can try the spell here. If it goes well, the brick will be somewhere on the outside. But I suspect the inside, at least the inside of the warehouse section, is going to be brick, too. We might have to break in to get it."

"Doll, the way this place is shooting off bad mojo, I'm guessing the brick is right out in the open."

"Me, too, but I want to be prepared."

"In that case, before you go casting your spell, I got something to say."

Max pulled his eyes away from the dark, tall warehouse windows and focused on Drummond. "What's wrong? Besides the obvious."

"All I'm suggesting here is that we take a breath to think this through. There's a lot of darkness here. We're all feeling it. Do we really want to get that brick and give it back to the coven? If this is the feeling we get from Grandma Mobley's spirit being in a brick, what'll she be like with it in her body? That's all. I'll follow what you want to do, but please listen to me for once and give this some thought."

The energy from the walls radiated against Max's skin like heat from a broiler. He looked into Sandra's eyes. Determination and surety gazed back at him.

To Drummond, he said, "Even if we agree with you, we can't leave it here."

"Why not?"

"Eventually, the Goodman hunters will find it. And while I won't mourn the loss of a coven in the world, I can't really wish death upon Grandma Mobley or Lena. I mean, it's one thing when they die in the midst of attempting to harm others, but this — this feels like murder."

"That's a bit extreme. Don't forget, these witches are the enemy. Like Hull and the Magi group, they all want to gain power over others. We're at war with them, and in a war, killing the enemy is not murder."

Max gestured to Sandra as she bent to the ground and, using a stick, drew a casting circle around herself. "You going to kill my wife because she casts spells?"

"Don't be ridiculous."

"But if she keeps learning about magic, keeps expanding her ability, then she'll essentially be a witch. I'm not too keen on it, but she wouldn't be hurting people and I think we both can agree that she'd use magic to stop other witches."

"You answered your own question. It's the greedy and evil witches we're after."

"What about the other coven witches that died? Was Candace evil? Or Laverne?"

Drummond shrugged. "We didn't kill them."

"But we don't know. We can never know truly unless we catch them in the act of doing bad. I mean, we saw with our own eyes the Goodman hunters murder Candace and kidnap Laverne. They've done crimes we witnessed. But what about the coven? We've seen nothing. The worst we can point to is that Grandma Mobley has lived an unnaturally long life. That's not magic I'm willing to murder someone over."

Turning his head away, Drummond said, "Look, I understand the position you're in. You've got to be in favor of witches because of your wife, but —"

"Wow. Really? You're going to blame this on her? I've spent the last several days yelling at her because I don't want her doing magic. Hell, in the past I've been tortured by witches, drugged by them, had my life spun out of control by them, and most recently, I've been cursed by them. Don't you dare start thinking I'm all in favor of witches. For that matter, you were in love with a witch once. And she was in a coven."

"That's why I kept telling you two to back out of this case. I've got experience in these matters."

Sandra stood. "Both of you, shut up. Here's what's going to happen. I'm casting this spell, and we're taking the brick. Max is right. We are not murderers, and Drummond, you know it. I know this case has gotten under your skin, but acting like a belligerent ass is not going to make it end any quicker." Sandra cocked her head to the side. "Who's that?"

Max whipped around to see a bald man with a flaming cross tattoo. The man started at the sight of them and dashed back around the corner of the building. To Drummond, Max said, "Watch her. There might be more of them."

"You got it."

To Sandra, he added, "Do the spell. Get the brick. I'll be right back."

She reached out for him. "Let him go." But Max had already started running.

Over his shoulder, he said, "Can't. He knows where the other brick is."

Chapter 24

MAX TURNED THE CORNER. The man had rushed down a full block before slowing to a normal walking pace. Though there were few pedestrians, Max still had to be careful. Plenty of cars and store owners were around. He couldn't apprehend the man in front of endless witnesses.

But he refused to let the man escape.

Though still walking, Max quickened his pace in an effort to close the distance. The man neared the crosswalk. Max's calves burned from the unusual gait required to keep from running. He wondered if the man had been listening to his argument with Drummond. But this man had caused enough hurt for a lifetime. For now, this was the real enemy.

The tattooed man stood at the crosswalk as cars zipped by. A bell dinged over and over. Red flashing lights of the railroad crossing signs kicked on and barrier arms lowered. Somewhere behind Max a locomotive blew its horn to signal its approach.

The thought hit Max — *a lucky break*. The man was stuck until the train passed. Except no — the man simply crossed the street and continued parallel to the tracks. With plenty of distraction as the freight train rolled by — boxcar after boxcar after tanker car after tanker car — the man broke into a jog.

Max gave up all pretenses. He dashed forward, closing in as fast as he could manage. The man glanced back, saw Max, and sprinted off across a gravel parking lot next to a tiny Mom-n-Pop diner.

As Max followed, he saw a thin area of trees with a few buildings peeking through. But he didn't see the man. Which meant he should have checked behind —

The man blitzed forward with his fist overhead. Without thinking, Max bent to the side and twisted away. This saved him from being clobbered in the head, but he still took a hard blow on the shoulder blade. He stumbled a few steps. With his adrenaline pumping, he whirled around, bringing his fists up, and setting his feet in a fighting stance.

"Aw, yeah," the man said with an odd accent Max couldn't place. "Let's have us a fistfight."

The man's muscular physique backed up his confidence, but Max had been learning how to hold his own. He knew he might not win the fight, but with his limited training, he might be able to hurt this man.

The man growled and cracked his knuckles. Max did not flinch. He put a light bounce to his legs, getting ready to move at the first sign of action.

Baldy — Max thought up the simple tag that instant — threw a few light jabs, not intended to hit but merely to get his distance and see how twitchy his opponent was. Max smirked. Not too twitchy at all — though inside, his nerves rattled like a frightened dog.

Again, Baldy jabbed. He grinned with such malice that Max knew the man had begun his career of pain by torturing ants with a magnifying glass as a kid, probably worked up to "disciplining" the family dog, and if he had somehow conned a woman into marrying him, she had suffered through a blackeye or two as well. Baldy shifted his feet and sent off two more jabs. Again, not seriously attempting to make contact.

But for all his swagger, Baldy had already made a mistake. Max noticed that right before each jab, the man lowered slightly as if he had to dip into the punch. The next time Baldy made that motion, Max acted.

Using one of his favorite moves from training, he blocked the jab with his forearm, striking from the outside inward. This knocked Baldy's jabbing arm aside and opened him up as an easy target. Max followed through the block, turning his body around to plant a solid back kick straight into Baldy's chest.

Max and Baldy paused, both astonished by the successful move. Then Baldy bared his teeth as his head flushed with anger. He roared as he barreled forward. But this did not deter

Max. He stayed calm and focused like a matador facing a charging bull. When the enraged man reached out for a tackle, Max sidestepped and aimed a punch for the man's lower ribs.

"We can stop this anytime," Max said, unable to suppress an arrogant roll of the shoulders. "I got a few questions, and I don't want to keep hurting you."

Spitting off to the side as he reset for more fighting, Baldy had lost the blind rage. He now approached like a seasoned fighter respecting his opponent. He kept inching closer, circling, waiting.

Not good, Max thought. It was easy to land hits against a man underestimating the fight. But with this change, Max knew Baldy would not go down with ease.

Baldy dipped as he launched into another attack, and Max stepped forward to block. Only this time, Baldy had faked the attack. He had baited Max into action and took full advantage of knowing where Max would end up.

The punches came fast and hard. Three to the side that lifted Max slightly off his feet and one to the face that left Max's head ringing. A tingling wave crashed through his body. He weaved backwards like a drunk, and Baldy rushed in for another strike. This time, he hit Max in the gut.

But martial arts training had taught Max a crucial lesson in fighting — *fighters get hit.* There was no way to avoid it. Max had spent enough time sparring that he had learned how to take a blow to the body and keep going.

When Baldy moved forward, Max snapped a sharp fist into the man's chin. Stunned by the unexpected attack, Baldy lost his momentum. Max followed up with a flurry of combinations — punches and kicks and whirling back into an elbow strike. Ending with a loud yell, Max stood tall as Baldy dropped to one knee and waved his hand.

"Okay, okay. Stop," Baldy said.

Before Baldy might look upward, Max closed his gaping mouth. He had won his first fistfight, and though he knew luck had played its part — a huge part — he still felt a touch of pride flowing through his veins.

"Over here," Drummond yelled to Sandra before darting over to Max. "Will you look at that? You sure kicked this guy in the rear."

Max winked at Drummond but kept at the ready in case Baldy decided to take a chance at escape. Sandra hustled toward them, the worry on her face dissipating with every step closer. A hint of a smile grew on her lips that Max had never seen before — and he thought he had seen them all.

"Any luck?" he asked.

She opened her purse and pulled out a brick. "Not hard at all. Didn't even need our friend to get it out. It practically popped out on its own."

"No *practically* about it," Drummond said. "I saw the thing respond to her touch. It wanted to come out."

When Baldy saw the brick, he bowed his head and laughed. "What is it with you people and those bricks?"

"Keep quiet," Max said, "or I'll have to hit you again."

"Good. I want you to."

"Huh?"

Keeping his head low — in fact, Max swore the man took care to cover his mouth in the crook of his arm — Baldy said, "I let you beat me. Don't you get it? I need you to hit me so I can pretend to be knocked out. Then you take me away in a car. Take me someplace safe, and I'll tell you everything."

Though the thoughts in Max's head swirled in a typhoon of gray cell connections, he also knew that he needed to act first. He'd make sense of it later. To Sandra, he said, "Get the car."

Baldy made a show of stumbling to his feet. "You'll never win!"

A bit over-the-top, but it gave Max all he required. With a swift motion, he clocked Baldy on the chin. This time, when the man fell over, Max lost all sense of accomplishment. He would keep training, but he could see by the dive the man took that he had much to learn.

Chapter 25

THEY DROVE BACK TO THEIR HOUSE and sat Baldy on a folding chair in the middle of the garage. Sandra wanted to interrogate him at the office, but Max warned that an office called The Porter Agency would be easier to find than their house address which would be listed with all the other Porters. He knew the argument sounded weak, but he didn't want Sandra catching PB carrying out his assignment, so he had to steer her away from the office.

At Drummond's insistence, they tied Baldy's hands behind his back. Baldy, whose real name turned out to be Bill Corte, did not resist. After they had him bound, Max said, "Time to talk."

"They told me about you folks. Told me you'd be trying to stop us. You're usually on the right side of things, but you're really working for witches. That's screwed up. Why are you trying to stop us from saving people from witches?"

Drummond snapped his fingers and pointed at the man. "That's a good question."

"If I've learned anything here in the South," Max said, "it's that oftentimes you've got to deal with one group you don't like in order to stop a more powerful group that means to do serious harm — if you even have a choice in the matter, at all."

Bill sneered. "But you work for Mother Hope and the Magi."

"We don't work for them. We have an arrangement. That's all."

"If it's anything like the arrangement I'm stuck in, you're a sorry sucker like me."

Sandra opened another folding chair and sat. "Tell us about your arrangement. Why are you working for the Goodman hunters?"

Bill's eyes widened. "It's not like that. I never even heard of Goodman and all that until a month ago. Shit, all the Goodman hunters never heard of the Goodman hunters until a few months before that. And I swear I never even knew witches were real. Honest. They recruited me and a few others, said they were getting the Goodman Witch Hunters back in action and needed young blood to do the fighting. I said I don't fight for free and they threw a lot of money at me."

"To go fight witches?"

"That's what they said. The kid running the thing comes from real money, and he tosses it around to get things done. I've roughed up guys for loan sharks before. I don't mind playing the muscle. And I didn't care if it was for imaginary creatures — as long as the money was real."

"But then you found out the witches were real, too."

He nodded, the growing fear of his new reality evident in his shocked eyes. "First couple times, I thought it was all a trick. Some weird way of keeping us all in line. But then I saw what happened to that one in the Science Center. I didn't sign up for that bullshit. All I wanted was to get paid for scaring a few ladies and a little vandalism. Next thing I know, I'm seeing actual magic spells going off in front of me. Last thing I heard, they're telling me ghosts are real, too. Can you believe that one?"

"Oh, I can," Max said as Drummond hovered over Bill.

"Then there's this." Bill pointed to his flaming cross tattoo. "When we joined, they threw a party, gave us beer and toasted our success. Turned out the beer had been drugged. When I woke, I had this tattooed on me. The boss came in and he warned us that we were now all cursed. If we ever told anybody about this stuff, if we ever told you guys specifically about this, then the curse would go off."

Sandra said, "But aren't you telling us now?"

"I didn't believe in any of this until the Science Center. I just want out, and no way are they letting me out. I figured, since witches and ghosts and all that is true, then maybe you all are true, too. They say you've faced down witches and worse, and you're still here, so I'm guessing you know what you're doing. Don't really have a choice, anyway, do I?"

Drummond floated a circle around Bill's head, staring down at him the entire time. "Y'know, I think this fella might be telling the truth. You should get every last bit of information you can from him."

"Tell me something," Max said. "How bad do you want out?"

"I don't want anything to do with any of this. The man can keep his money. I'll leave town if that's what's necessary. I've seen more than I ever want to."

"We can help you. But we need you to answer a few more questions."

"Anything. Ask away."

"Who's running the Goodman hunters?"

Bill bent forward and winced. Max thought perhaps he had broken the man's rib, but then Bill took a sharp breath and straightened. "Grant Felder. He's the head of the hunters."

"Who the heck is Grant Felder?" Drummond asked.

Sandra glanced at Max, and he shrugged. He said the name several times in his head to remember it. More research for later, perhaps. *Don't be stupid, Max*, he thought. He had the perfect prime source sitting in front of him.

"Tell us about Grant Felder."

Bill said, "He's a card shark that I knew for a few years. Never was great at it, but he managed to get by. His dad or granddad or whatever was part of the Goodman hunters and the old man had plenty of cash. Felder, he brought me in on all of this. Found me at a bar, got me drunk, and said it'd be perfect for what I'm good at, said the rest of the old timers were gone, but he wanted to bring it all back for his dad. Something like that, anyway. I was drunk."

"Seems a lot of bad things happen to you when you drink."

"Yeah, I'll look into AA right away. Meanwhile, I think I'll try not to die from a witch and her gang. You going to help me or what?"

"What witch?"

"I told you already — they cursed me with this tattoo."

"You said that Felder did that, meaning he's got a witch."

"Why would Felder work with a witch? He's leading up the Goodman Witch Hunters. As in hunt and kill."

"Bill," Sandra said, her voice soft, calm, and full of menace. "I'm a witch. And I'm capable of a lot you don't want to see. So, stop jerking us around and start explaining things. Who are you talking about?"

Bill looked up and Max offered only confirmation. The bald man's face dropped and his eyes glistened with tears. "Grant is the money, but really he's nothing but a middle man."

"Then who's the real man behind the curtain?"

He swallowed dry and winced as if the name caused him pain. "Leon Moore."

"What?" Max blurted out. "You're telling me that Leon Moore of the Magi hired you?"

"Yeah. Big black fellow. Works for a witch. He's the only one we've dealt with but I heard stories about her and the Magi."

Sandra walked next to Max. "Leon Moore restarted the Goodman hunters?"

"That's right. He told us the truth about witches, told us about this one group of them, this coven, and he showed us how to properly destroy the bricks so that they'll be killed."

Sandra went on, "Did he also show you how to find the bricks? Or did he have a list or something?"

"That's all Grant's job. He's the one that finds the bricks, and he's the one that tells the rest of the hunters what to do. I never asked how he did it, but I'm pretty sure Leon Moore showed him."

Max looked at Sandra and Drummond as they all let Bill's words sink in.

Bill watched them, his body tensing. "You gotta believe me. I told you what I know, and this curse — that's why I had to put on that show. Let you beat me up and take me away. They're always watching me. They said if I ever talked, then the curse would go off. It's going to happen soon. You said you'd help me get out of this." He looked straight at Sandra. "You. You said you're a witch. Get this off of me. De-curse me."

"One more question," Max said, "and then we'll help you. The brick you guys stole but didn't destroy. Where is it?"

"I don't have it. I swear. I didn't want that thing near me. You can feel it's not right."

"I didn't say you had it. I asked where it is. Who has it? Grant Felder?"

"That prick is all big on showing off how tough he is, but he ain't ever thrown a punch in his life. He wouldn't go near the bricks other than to point out which one we needed to get. No, the brick is where you'd expect it to be. We gave it to him."

"To who?"

"You know who. Look, I shouldn't keep saying his name. It's like calling the curse upon me."

"Leon Moore has the brick. That's what you're afraid to say."

"Yeah, yeah. Alright? Leon Moore. Satisfied?"

Before the last syllable had left his mouth, Bill lurched off the chair onto his knees. His lips formed a large O as his throat convulsed. Max grabbed a trash can from the side of the garage and brought it over but by the time he reached Bill, the man's face had relaxed.

"You okay?" Max asked.

Bill raised his head slowly like a monk who had finally meditated his way into enlightenment — except darkness and shadow accompanied Bill's newfound knowledge. "I've been stupid this whole time. I thought you'd really be able to help me."

"We will. We'll try, at least. My wife knows a lot about magic. If there's a way to break that curse on you, she'll —"

"I can feel the heat rising. I should've known that it wouldn't matter if they could see me or not. The curse knows. It's all real, and I knew it from the start but I denied it. I pretended, but you know what? Just because you deny gravity, doesn't mean you can fly. The curse knows that I betrayed them. And there's nothing anybody can do now. I have to pay for it."

He arched back as if stricken by a cattle prod, his mouth wide open, and a strained gurgling clicked in his throat. Sandra moved in, but Max grabbed her arm and pulled her back.

"Look," Drummond said. "The tattoo."

The dark outline of the flaming cross glowed like embers. With an audible pop, the tattoo burst into real flames. Bill moaned as the fire spread up his arm. Tears streamed down his face and he cried out a long howl.

The fire spread fast across his skin, burst out from within his bones and muscles. Sparks shot out of his mouth. A putrid smoke rose above him, dark and foul, reeking of death.

Max rushed into the house, bolted to the living room, swiped a blanket from the couch, and hurried back. But as he reached the kitchen, the howling cries ceased. He slammed back into the garage and halted.

A fiery ball of orange and yellow burned in the middle of the concrete floor. Sandra opened the garage door so they didn't suffocate from smoke inhalation as Max covered Bill with the blanket. But when he pulled back, the blanket fell flat on the ground.

Max picked it up. Only ash remained. No clothing, no hair, no bone — nothing but ash.

Chapter 26

MAX AND SANDRA SAT IN THEIR CAR parked in the driveway. They had closed the garage door, and both simply stared out the windshield. Neither wanted to be in the house at the moment — maybe not for a long time to come.

A queasy sensation rolled up from Max's stomach. "This is a whole new level of twisted."

Max forced himself to think of happier times — his wedding, his wedding night, their first date — anything to wash away the terrible sight stuck on repeat in his brain. But the second he let his mind relax, he saw the flames again, he heard the cries, he smelled the charred death.

"We're going to have to sell this place and find a new house," Max said.

Sandra did not respond. But after a few minutes of quiet, she said, "This is our fault."

"How?"

"He showed us the curse. He told us he was afraid. I should've immediately started looking into it. We were so eager for information that we never once thought to help him first."

"There's no way we could've known that would happen. I've been cursed for a long time now and nothing's happened to me."

"Not yet."

"We had no way to know that his curse would enact so fast."

"Sure, we did. We just had to research a little instead of pressuring him to answer our questions."

Drummond slid through the garage door and settled in the back of the car. "I've looked over every inch of your house. I don't see anything that suggests the Magi put a ward or curse or marker on the property. I think we're safe to assume that the tattoo itself was the only connection this curse had to Bill Corte. Which means that the Magi know he talked to somebody, but they don't know who."

Max knocked his knuckles on his forehead. "Who else would he be talking to?"

"Fair enough. I'll amend my statement — they can only presume."

"What the hell are we going to do now? This is so messed up."

Sandra gave a firm nod. Max perked up. He knew that nod — she had confirmed something in her own mind.

"We have the last brick," she said. "We deliver it to the Mobley Coven and we walk away."

"There's still another brick out there."

"Not our problem. And if they want to hire us to find that one, we politely tell them that we've got other clients to work with." Not bothering to let Max ask the obvious question, she continued, "Like you said — what we've seen just now is a whole new level of twisted. Something about these bricks scares Mother Hope enough to cause this kind of damage — to target these men, recruit them into the Goodman hunters, drug them, curse them, and then let them die in such a horrible way — whatever is going on between the Magi and the Mobley Coven, we don't want anything more to do with it."

Drummond clapped his hands once. "There we go. I've finally got the missus onboard with common sense when dealing with a coven. So, how about it? Let's be done with it all."

Taking Max by the hand, Sandra said, "And yes, hon, we can sell the house. I don't want to live around the kind of negative residual spirit Bill most likely left behind. No way."

Max merely stared into space. "You're right," he said. Everything Sandra had said entered his head but his thoughts tumbled over each other too fast to speak about. Things clicked together in ways he had not seen before. "This is all about Mother Hope."

Drummond said, "I know what you're doing. Just stop it. The case is over. Done. We're giving the brick to the witch — not the best idea, but with the Goodman hunters holding the other brick, I'm not too worried. We do that and we walk away. Fully intact. Not burned to a crisp like Bill Corte. Okay? Can we all agree on that simple line of action for once?"

Max started the car. "Sorry, but this is more than just a brick."

"Of course, it is." Drummond threw his hat out the window, slumped back, and waited for it to reappear on his head.

"You wanted to go return the brick. That's what we're going to do."

"Yeah, but I want to return and leave."

"Not until we have the full truth. I think I know what's going on and it's not something we can walk away from."

Sandra's hands slid over her purse with the brick. "You going to let us in on it?"

As Max reversed out of the driveway, he said, "You said it yourself. Mother Hope went out of her way to cause this damage. Why? It's got to be the same reason she does anything."

Drummond shot forward, his eyes lighting up. "You think this is some kind of power grab?"

"That's what we're going to find out."

Chapter 27

MAX HOPED THIS WOULD BE THE LAST TIME he ever set foot in the Mobley Coven's house. They had called ahead from the car, so Lena prepared coffee and waited for them in the same room where this case had begun — same light curtains, same plush couch, same thick carpeting, same cute knick-knacks, and the same warm paintings. All to present the image of an average, suburban home.

Except for the woman over one hundred years old, half dead, and sitting in a wheelchair by the fireplace.

Except for the anxious, jackhammering knees of Lena Mobley.

Except for the nine other women standing at the back, watching every motion, listening to every whisper.

Yeah, other than all of that, Max thought they pulled off average, suburban home perfectly.

As Max and Sandra lowered onto the couch, Drummond stood behind them and eyed all of the coven. "I know this goes without saying, but I've got to say it. Max, watch the smart-ass comments. You're facing an entire coven."

Max refrained from turning around and making a smart-ass comment. Instead, he smiled at Lena. "Thank you for seeing us on short notice. We've got good and bad news."

Lena gestured to the witches behind her. "You didn't think I convened them all here because I thought you wanted to chat about the weather. Your wife said you were on your way and that you had a brick for us. *The* brick."

Sandra pulled the brick from her purse and all the witches inched forward. She placed the brick on the coffee table. "Unfortunately, the Goodman hunters beat us to the other remaining brick. That's the bad news. One of you is still in danger."

Lena placed the tips of her fingers on either side and raised the brick. One witch stepped forward with a silver tray, and Lena set the brick on the tray like a chemist holding a flask of volatile liquids. The witch stepped back with the others, and though Max tried to keep an eye on the brick, he quickly lost sight of it. The witches stood still as if nothing had happened. Whatever they had done, Max figured that brick would never be seen again.

"This brick is the insurance we need to protect Grandma Mobley's future. The other brick — we hope to recover it, our coven has suffered enough loss, but we are all willing to make the sacrifice for the coven and for Grandma Mobley. Especially myself. There is no other death that could be more meaningful to me or any of us."

"Maybe we can arrange that," Drummond said, and Max glanced back at him. "What? I said *you* shouldn't make smart-ass comments. She can't hear me. I can say all I want."

Without a noticeable signal, a middle-aged, Chinese witch from the back walked up to Lena's side, made a slight bow, and handed her a thick envelope. As the witch backed away, Lena placed the envelope on the coffee table and pushed it over. "You've both done well. Consider that a bonus to the fee we already paid. We like to show appreciation when it is deserved, and without your help, we most likely would have been destroyed as a coven."

"Happy to oblige," Max said as he took the envelope and slipped it into his pocket.

"Unless there is anything else you have to report, I think this matter has been put to rest. You may leave, and with any luck, we will never be in a position to call upon your services again."

"Gee whiz," Drummond said. "Thanks for your permission. Should we curtsy before we go?"

Sandra shook hands with Lena. "Thank you for the opportunity. I only wish we could have been more successful. I'm sure Candace and Laverne were lovely women."

"That's kind of you. Thank you."

"Yeah," Max said, patting his pursed lips as he stood. "About all of this. I still have a few questions."

"Oh?" Lena glanced at the withering face of Grandma Mobley.

Max paced around the couch, rarely looking beyond his own thoughts. "This case has been weird from the start. I mean the fact that you contacted us in the first place seems a bit weird."

"We didn't want the police involved and your agency is the only one with the necessary experience."

"Put it like that and it makes plenty of sense. But only if you ignore the obvious question — why hire anybody at all?"

Lena reared back as if looking at an alien species. "Our beloved sister Laverne was missing. Why wouldn't we hire somebody to help find her?"

"For one thing, you had an entire coven at your disposal. Surely, more than a few of these women could have cast a spell to locate Laverne. Isn't that right, ladies? Raise your hand if you'd have been willing to put your life on the line for Laverne?"

None raised their hands. They were too busy shooting confused glares at Lena.

"Mr. Porter, what are you trying to imply?"

"I'm merely asking a few questions so that we can close this case with the full truth."

"You weren't hired to find the full truth. Just to recover the bricks."

Drummond snickered. "I love seeing when your brain does this. Savor the moment, pal, and get this witch to confess whatever she did."

Ignoring the echoes of a witch hunt, Max said, "I thought we were hired to save Laverne, then Candace, and only then did it become about getting the bricks. Unless, of course, it was always about getting the bricks. Your fellow witches never really figured into it, did they? I mean, you said it yourself, all of you are ready to sacrifice your lives for this coven. Right, ladies?"

Lena stood. "I'm afraid I must ask you to leave."

"But I have some more questions."

"It's clear your intent is to foment discord within our group. That will not be tolerated."

Shaking his finger at the side of his head, Max said, "I'm only trying to get honest answers. Get the truth. Because here's the thing — nothing you've said or done makes any sense with the idea of hiring us. That's the part that keeps bothering me. See, we learned that the Goodman Witch Hunters have only recently reformed and all of that was due to them being hired by a third party. Now, it's obvious to us that this third party did this hiring because — well, truthfully, they bribed, coerced, and cursed the hunters — but they did it all to put some distance between their group and the actions they wanted the hunters to take. That got me thinking. Why did you hire us? Why not take care of things yourself? Unless you were doing the same thing."

Lena wrinkled her nose with a cross look. "Each sister in the coven has duties and responsibilities. One of my main functions is to protect ourselves from unwanted discovery. No coven worth anything, no coven with any real power, manages to last long by being out in the open."

"Especially back in the Hull days."

"Exactly. When events require us to maneuver in a more public way, we've learned through the decades that it is best to hired qualified assistance."

"That would be us?"

"Naturally."

Max rubbed his chin as he winked at Sandra. "Are you buying any of this?"

She thought it over. "It makes a little sense. Witches don't have a good track record of getting along with the rest of the world."

Lena's shoulders eased slightly. "Thank you."

"Only problem I see is that there wasn't any need for you to deal with the public at all. You knew about the bricks, you knew everything that was going on. As my husband pointed out, you have numerous witches at your disposal, and if the rumors are true, you are the most powerful coven around. That means your witches are the most powerful. Surely, they could have handled all of this with a few choice spells cast in the night away from prying eyes."

Max pecked Sandra's cheek. Sitting back on the couch, he said, "She's right except for one thing. My wife said that your witches are the most powerful. But there's one powerful witch that, I'm guessing, is a notch above all of you — Mother Hope."

The entire coven hushed a gasp at the name.

Like an old schoolmarm, Lena pointed a sharp finger at the door. "You will leave now or you'll see just how powerful we are."

But Grandma Mobley lifted her hand. Slow, shaking, and causing her face to grimace, she gestured Lena over. Lena glowered at Max as she crossed the room. Grandma Mobley whispered to Lena and finished with a harsh cough that had all of the coven sisters watching with worry.

Lena returned to her chair. Her mouth had tightened into a sharp dot, and her nostrils flared like a dragon holding back the fire in its belly. "It seems we are going to tell you the full truth."

Though Max knew he had won this battle of words, his nerves sent tremors across his skin. He feared he wouldn't like the reward.

Chapter 28

ALTHOUGH THE AIR CONDITIONING BLASTED through the vents, Max still felt sweat dampening his body. He figured part of that came from having eleven witches, Sandra, himself, and a ghost all packed into a cozy living room. But part of it came from the way Grandma Mobley turned a milky eye upon him. And part of it came from Lena taking the time to walk into the kitchen, return with a bottle of rum, and pouring a strong dose into her coffee.

She set the bottle on the table and sat back with her spiked drink. "Where to begin?"

"That depends." Max crossed his legs as if he had no care for how long her story dragged into the night. "How long has the Mobley Coven been at war with the Magi?"

"No, no, Mr. Porter. It goes far deeper than that."

Sandra said, "Perhaps you should begin with whatever started this ... *feud?*"

"An excellent word. Fairly accurate."

Grandma Mobley groaned as she jutted her chin toward Lena. Two of the coven hastened forward to be at the old woman's side. Lena, on the other hand, appeared to shrink under that dark gaze.

Max said, "Looks like Grandma Mobley wants you to get to the point."

"I suppose," Lena said, "the sooner I get this over with, the sooner you'll be out of our lives. Pay attention. I will not be repeating the details."

"You have our full attention."

Drummond said, "Not mine. I'm keeping my focus on the rest of the coven. It'd be just like witches to get you wrapped up in a tale while the others cast some curse on you. Don't worry, though, I've got you both covered."

While Max did not think the coven would do such a thing at this time, not when Grandma Mobley made it clear she wanted the truth outed, he still appreciated having Drummond to keep an eye on the bigger picture. It put Max at ease — well, at less tension than when he had entered the house.

Lena sipped her coffee as she gathered her thoughts, and then set it on the table with a soft clink. "Just like Grandma Mobley, your Mother Hope has remained alive a long time. Longer than is natural. The number of witches who have successfully achieved that level of control over magic can be counted on one hand. Their successes were done by different means, but the result is similar."

Max kept silent, but he wanted to point out that Mother Hope's condition far exceeded that of Grandma Mobley. Although, he wondered if there might be bricks or other objects out there with Mother Hope's spirit locked away.

"It should not be surprising, then," Lena went on, "that these two formidable women would come into contact with each other. The first time occurred in 1907. Mother Hope had been traveling throughout the South, and she had taken up lodging in Old Salem. By this point in time, Grandma Mobley had begun assembling more and more powerful witches to work with her. She had a network of information gatherers —"

Drummond said, "She means spies."

"— and they told her of Mother Hope. Grandma Mobley had heard stories about the powerful witch Hope and thought this woman — every bit as brave and smart and audacious as herself — would be the perfect addition. In fact, had Mother Hope joined Grandma Mobley, in all likelihood they would have easily destroyed the Hull family and taken control of North Carolina magic. But that is not what happened. Mother Hope had already begun to reject the true spirit within her. It would still be some years before the Magi were officially formed, but she had begun to walk that road." She took another swig of her special coffee. "When Grandma Mobley invited the young Hope to dinner and presented her ideas, particularly focusing on removing the Hulls from power, Mother Hope declined politely. But by all accounts we have, and by Grandma Mobley's own recollection, the two witches knew right away that they would forever be enemies. Neither said it directly, but they knew.

"Now, in itself, that is not a surprising matter. Witches often act like owners of competing businesses. Everyone wants to stake out their territory and as long as they don't feel that another is encroaching on them, all is well. But, of course, somebody is always taking a piece of what you think belongs to you. When you live as long as these two women have, the opportunity to foul each other's territory, by intent or mistake, is compounded.

"Over the next several decades, they tried to avoid each other. Then over the decades after, they went out of their way to harm each other. Grandma Mobley sought a quiet gain in power through better and better witchcraft in the coven as well as seeking out ways to rid herself of the Hulls. No matter how much sense it made that she and Mother Hope should work together against the Hulls, Mother Hope would not have it. In her eyes, Grandma Mobley was an evil witch and deserved nothing.

"Mother Hope likes to paint herself as a martyr of witches, a holier-than-thou type that would never misuse the power she acquired. But one look at her behavior since the destruction of the Hull family proves how corrupt she is."

Max said, "I think I'm getting a very clear picture. Grandma Mobley and all of you, her beloved coven, you all have done a remarkable job staying hidden. The Hulls must have known about you, but either they were always distracted by bigger problems or they underestimated how strong you all had become."

"We may have used some magic to nudge them one way or another at times."

"I'll bet. And though you all despise Mother Hope and the Magi, you figured she would only be setting herself up for a fall by taking on Hull. So, you sat back and let her attract all the attention. Except things changed."

Sandra faced Max as the truth dawned over her. "We came into the picture."

"That's right. We moved to Winston-Salem and started causing ripples throughout the entire community. Nobody, not even the Hulls, could have predicted how our actions would alter things. And certainly none of the Mobley Coven could believe that with our interference somehow Mother Hope would be part of taking down the Hulls. But that's exactly what happened."

Lena said, "I'm glad you see how complicit you are in creating the current situation."

"Not that you object."

"You really do understand now, don't you?"

Drummond crossed his arms. "Well, I don't."

Max could not hide his amazement. So much that had happened in Winston-Salem during the last few years all traced back to their arrival in the city. As his wife had wisely said — like ripples.

"You had been waiting for many years," Max said. "Grandma Mobley even longer. But despite all that time being patient, you never could really plan ahead because you never knew what or who would destroy the Hulls. You had no idea what shape the world would take afterwards. Mother Hope being at the center of it must have been one of your worst-case scenarios. Especially because she moved fast to consolidate her power. Much faster than you."

"We had to fix our vulnerability first."

A short laugh erupted from Max's chest. "Oh, wow. You really were unprepared. You had to get those bricks before anybody else found out. And then Mother Hope started to move in on you. She had dealt with all the other challenges to her authority, and now it was down to you. Big dog versus big dog."

Sandra's mouth dropped open. "You're saying all of this was just a power grab?"

"It's more than power," Lena said, rising in her chair. "It's controlling the use of magic in the area to make sure that we are all protected. That's what Mother Hope will never see and what the Hulls abused."

"Protected? Aren't you the most powerful coven?"

"To take control of the area means to protect all the witches. To govern them so that we never suffer from an actual witch hunt. These days, the public is generally skeptical that we have any real power, and that's part of the job — keeping it that way. Because if they ever knew the truth, all the old fears would resurface like a hurricane. Vigilantes would appear overnight. Witches would be dragged from their homes and hung like in Salem or burned at the stake like in Europe. Many innocent women would fall to that fate as well. Homes would be split apart, and children would be ostracized. There would be chaos unleashed, and neither side would benefit. That is why we want to see that Mother Hope and the Magi do not gain full control."

Max's brow drew down. "Part of this still doesn't click together. Not anything about you or the coven. The problem that I'm having is with Mother Hope."

"Isn't she always the problem?" Drummond said.

"I'm not sure why she hasn't destroyed you all yet."

The entire coven stared at Max.

"If you think about it," he continued, "she had all the cards going into this. She obviously found out about the bricks, she set up the Goodman hunters to hide her involvement and any possible retaliation, and then she systematically started killing you. Our involvement caused some problems — that's why Leon Moore attempted to bully me off the case — but I don't see how we turned the tide. They have a brick, and they've been watching you. So why didn't they kidnap one of you and destroy the brick? Why this drawn out way of handling things? Heck, why didn't she organize three dozen men and lay siege to this house?"

Nobody spoke as Max's words settled in the air.

"It's Leon Moore," Sandra said, jumping to her feet. "We've been thinking about him all wrong."

"What are you talking about?"

Sandra weaved around Max's knees, the coffee table, and one of the witches until she stood directly in front of Grandma Mobley. "You and Mother Hope know all about each other. That's what you've had Lena telling us. So that means you know about the curse she put on my husband."

Max's hope skyrocketed only to be blown to pieces when Lena said, "We can't break that curse. Nobody can."

Over her shoulder, Sandra said, "I will. Someday. For now, I only need the help from your coven, so you can help yourselves."

"Hon?" Max said, pulling on her sleeve like a child. "What's going on?"

"It's Leon. The reason the Magi have handled this so poorly and in such a weird way — with the Goodman hunters and all of that — it's because of Leon."

Max's whole body tingled as he saw what she meant. "They don't know. Mother Hope and the Magi — they aren't part of this. Leon is acting on his own."

She grabbed his hand. "We're going to get him." Back to Grandma Mobley. "May I have your help?"

The old woman closed her eyes as she gave a slight nod. Lena said, "You have your answer. We will help you. What can we do?"

"We need to make an amulet. And then I'll need some help casting a spell."

"Certainly. How many of our witches do you need for the spell?"

Sandra paused as she thought through her idea. "All of them."

Chapter 29

DRIVING UP MAIN STREET IN HIGH POINT looked like driving up Main Street in most small towns in the United States. Certainly not much different from Thomasville except no railroad tracks and no giant chair. But one block over, Max came upon the bus terminal — bright curving metal forming a large arching overhang over the roadway led to more modern architecture for the main part of the terminal. Max parked in a nearby lot.

Two buses idled beneath the overhang while passengers mulled about waiting for the departure call. Sunlight bounced through tinted skylights bathing the grounds in an unnatural green. Seemed fitting enough to Max — nothing natural was about to happen.

The night before, after Sandra shared her revelation regarding Leon Moore, the witches of the Mobley Coven got to work on the amulet. Sandra laid out her plan and received a shaky but affirmative nod from Grandma Mobley. Max caught a flicker of pride that crossed Sandra's face.

Lena, however, did not share the old woman's confidence. "You're welcome to use our library, but the kind of spell you want to cast is not something I've ever heard about."

"I have," Sandra said. "My husband is an expert at research and I've learned a lot from him. Over the last few years, I've studied and researched witchcraft in depth. I know this is possible. And since the Mobley Coven, the Coven of the Carolinas, is the most powerful coven around, surely your library will have the books we need. After all, it was Grandma Mobley who cast an incredibly rare and difficult spell so long ago that caused most of your current problems. Who else around here would amass books equally rare?"

"There's always a difference between what you read and what you can actually accomplish."

"That's why I have your entire coven to help."

Over the remainder of the night, Max assisted Sandra and Lena in the library — a section of the basement that had been finished off, lined with bookshelves, and filled with old volumes of ancient lore, spells, and history. Max loved it. He hated the reason behind it and he hated what he knew would be coming once the sun rose, but while the night continued, he immersed in the textures and aromas of the old books — many of them handwritten.

Drummond opted for sentry duty. Claiming he wanted to be ready should Leon Moore decide to strike first, he circled the house hour after hour. Max suspected the old ghost simply didn't want to spend that much time stuck near a witch coven.

Lena found the first entry they needed and Max located a later version of the spell that included several refinements. Sandra discovered the second entry required. However, none of them could figure out how to synthesize the two together. Then Grandma Mobley sent young Jessica down with a small, leatherbound book.

The way Lena held it — with reverence and shock — quieted the already silent room. "This is Grandma Mobley's personal journal. I've never held it before. It contains all the spells she developed in private. She told me that these were natural conclusions but nothing she dared to share for fear of what witches might do with it." Lena locked eyes with Sandra. "She wrote it with her own blood."

Max left the two women to put the spells together. That stepped beyond research and into the practical side of witchcraft. He would be no help there.

When dawn arrived, the time to call Leon had come. He did not have to say much. "I think we need to talk about the Goodman Witch Hunters."

That got Leon's attention. When he suggested the bus terminal, Max knew Sandra's conclusions were on target. The only reason to meet at the High Point bus terminal was to meet without Mother Hope or the Magi knowing about it. After all, if the Magi were involved, Leon would have wanted to meet on home turf — the O'Henry Hotel in Greensboro.

An hour later and Max walked beneath the bus terminal overhang with an amulet under his shirt and bouncing against his chest. Leon Moore sat at a bench amongst the bus travelers. He wore a tan jacket and brown pants and had a folded newspaper under his arm like an old timer people-watching to whittle away the day.

Drummond appeared at Max's side. "The ladies are getting ready," he said. "You should see your wife. She's like a General ordering the ranks in that house. You'd never know Lena or Grandma Mobley ever had any command at all."

Speaking out of the side of his mouth, Max said, "Keep the updates coming. You're the key to all of this." He meant it, too. Since Max and Sandra could both communicate with Drummond, he became the conduit between Max in High Point and Sandra in Winston-Salem. Without the ghost being able to use the Other to travel fast between locations, the plan would never have worked. For that matter, Sandra would never have come up with such a crazy idea. The closer Max walked toward Leon, the crazier the idea felt.

"Don't worry," Drummond said. "Everybody's working hard to see you through this safely."

Max's stomach churned. He willed his hands to his sides. He didn't want to involuntarily reach up and touch the amulet under his shirt. Giving that away would ruin everything.

Leon spotted him, offered a friendly wave, and scooted over to make room on the bench. "Always good to see you."

"I doubt that," Max said as he sat.

"Let's not be antagonistic about this. We've been on the same side often enough. This is a confusing, muddled part of the world we inhabit. I mean look at me — a few years ago, I was a broken old man shuffling through a library job they wanted to kick me out of. And I had only a few good years of eyesight left." Leon tapped Max with the newspaper. "And here's a secret you didn't know — I had cancer. Yup. The big

C. Pretty much thought I'd be dead by now. Then along comes you and the Hulls and then, of course, Mother Hope and the Magi. Well, that changed everything for me."

As Leon rambled, Max scanned the area as best as he could from his position. There were about twenty people standing around. A few smoked cigarettes while others read books. A mother crouched before her daughter making some silly joke the girl laughed at. Drummond drifted around the waiting area, making a more thorough check.

"You worked for the Magi long before I showed up," Max said.

"Not really. It's true I was associated with them, but it wasn't until you came along and shook everybody up that the opportunities came to me. It wasn't until then that Mother Hope saw my value. And of course, she healed me."

"Made you younger, too."

"It's a tradeoff. If I wasn't going to die, I might not have agreed."

"Deals with witches can be like that. You've got to be careful."

"With most witches, that's true. But with Mother Hope — well, she has a vision for our future that is beautiful. A world where witches don't have to deny who they are, don't have to fear being abused, don't have to live in the shadows. That's all she's after."

"The curse she put on me begs to differ. Remember this curse? If I piss her off enough, she can turn it on and I fall into a coma. My ghost gets trapped, tethered to my body, unable to move on but unable to return to the living. Doesn't seem like a beautiful vision of peace and harmony to me."

Leon crossed his legs. "I know you don't see what I see. That's okay. You'll just have to trust me on this one. I promise you — one day, once the peace she seeks is created, she'll free you of that curse."

Drummond appeared in front of Max. "I've looked around here. There's a ton of suspicious people but we're at a bus terminal. Suspicious people are not uncommon. Are you good for a few minutes? I want to check with Sandra to see how much longer until the spell is ready."

Max covered his mouth with his fist and coughed once. They had opted for standard and simple signals — one cough for yes, two for no. Drummond flicked the brim of his hat and disappeared.

"Even if I were to believe you," Max said to Leon, "there is still a gaping hole in the whole thing."

Leon laughed. "Just one? Look here, I'm no Spring chicken. I completely understand the difference between an ideal and reality. But it's important to embrace the ideal so that you can do everything in your power to make it reality. You think socialists and communists and capitalists and any other -ists are happy with the world as it is? They all strive for an ideal that will never come to be. You know why?"

"I do. But I'm sure you'll tell me anyway."

With a wink, Leon continued, "You're knife-edged sharp today. Well, yes, I'll tell you — the reason is greed. That's where all the corruption comes from. Greed for money or power or both. It ruins everything. Even if I were a dictator, greed would undermine my control over others. There would always be somebody willing to sell me out if the money offered was high enough. But even on a smaller level — not running a country or a state but simply attempting to protect the witches and supernatural from discovery — well, that's the ideal and the reality is always hampered by greed."

"You got that right. Only this time, it's your greed."

"Mine?"

"You've been sitting at Mother Hope's side for a while now. You've seen the different groups attempt to take over control. And as she's fought each attack off, she's gained more power — to the point that she can curse me without fear of repercussions. She's becoming judge, jury, and executioner. I think you started to see that Mother Hope had succumbed to the greed for power. She's strayed from the ideal you wanted to help her achieve. Especially when it came to the Mobley Coven."

"Is that what you think?"

"No point in denying it. I know you bribed Grant Felder into reforming the Goodman hunters. You hired muscle and then cursed them all so you could control them — perhaps your own greed for power really kicked in then. Must have felt good to hold all their lives in your hands. You then used them as a front to hide the fact that you wanted to destroy the Mobley Coven."

Drummond reappeared. "All is going well. You wouldn't believe the sight, though. They got an empty attic and a huge casting circle drawn on the floor. Took them a bit to get Grandma Mobley up there, but now the whole coven is around that circle and they've started the spell. Hang in there. It'll be ready pretty soon."

"Is that all?" Leon said. "Nothing more to say?"

"Only that I know you've been playing with witchcraft. Must be hard to stay away from the stuff when Mother Hope has all the best books sitting around in front of you just asking to be read. But the kinds of spells you're casting — things dealing with Grandma Mobley's spirit — that's dangerous. You're a child playing with a high voltage wire."

Drummond did a fast survey of the area. "Still tough to see anybody that might be working with him. I'm sure they're here, though. You need anything?"

Max coughed twice.

"Then I'm going back to the coven. Sandra said that once they complete the casting, you'll only have a few minutes at most to succeed. The second they're ready, I'll let you know. Until then, keep stalling."

Max coughed once and watched as the ghost vanished. Behind the spot where Drummond had been, a bus hissed and pulled away, and behind the bus, standing in the glow of the morning sun, Max saw a man dressed in black jeans and a black, short-sleeve shirt. The man had a tattoo on his forearm — a flaming cross.

Leon stood and stepped in front of Max. "Over the years since we first met, I've had the opportunity to watch you in action numerous times. You may dismiss this as an old black man's opinion, but I'm going to tell you something here — you ain't as smart as you think you are. I'm not saying you're dumb. But you're luckier than you'd like to admit."

"I'm a firm believer in the adage that the harder you work, the luckier you get." Though Max felt decidedly unlucky at the moment. From either side, he noticed men dressed all in black approaching. Though he dared not take the time to inspect closer, he had no doubt both men sported flaming cross tattoos. "So, this is how you all work? I speak the truth and you're going to beat me up."

"We're not going to beat you up. And your conclusions are speculation, not the truth."

"Then tell me the truth. I'm here because you failed in what you attempted, and clearly you don't want Mother Hope finding out about it. Let's talk. I'm sure we can come to some kind of solution for all involved."

Leon tucked his newspaper back under his arm. "Oh, don't worry about that. We're going to talk. But I think it's time to move this to a more private setting."

Max tried to rise, but the men on his sides pushed him back into the seat. He tried to look past Leon, tried to find Drummond, but the ghost had not returned yet. If Max left with Leon and the Goodman hunters, Sandra's plan would fall apart. They wouldn't know how to find Max, and as he understood it, the coven needed to know his location in order for the spell to be effective.

"Wait," he said as the men closed tighter around him. "I came here in good faith to talk with you. If you do this, if you take me against my will, you betray everything you stand for."

"Did you think that up on the spot?" Leon glanced around the bus terminal. "I'm impressed. It almost sounds logical. If I were dumb, I might have fallen for that — or at least paused long enough to ponder it. But I'm not dumb."

Something caught Leon's attention, something behind Max.

"Let's discuss this. If you —"

"Take him," Leon said. A black cloth hood went over Max's

head. Strong hands locked down his arms and yanked him to his feet. Though he could see nothing and could only hear his heavy breathing underneath the hood, he tried to keep moving with them. He imagined the Goodman hunters surrounded him and blocked him from view.

Nobody standing around would see anything but a group of tough-looking, similarly dressed men walking in a pack. People would assume they were a gang and would want nothing to do with them.

Max heard the sliding door of a van. A hand pressed his head down while another shoved him in. Before the door had fully slid shut, the engine revved and they were driving away.

Chapter 30

THE DRIVE SEEMED TO GO ON FOREVER. Max attempted the trick he had seen in spy movies many times — keeping his senses alert for every possible clue as to where they headed. He heard car radios and trucks. He felt the van accelerate to highway speeds. He smelled foods and exhaust. But it proved far more difficult to take that information and form a coherent travel path.

Besides, what did it matter? If Drummond somehow found him, there would be no need to say where he was being held. And if Drummond didn't find him — Max did not want to think about that.

At length, the van stopped. They led Max out and escorted him along a pebble-strewn path. A fresh pine aroma and the lacking sounds of civilization told Max they were in a forest. They climbed a few wooden steps and entered a building. Two hands thrust Max down into a chair and then bound his hands to the chair arms.

When they pulled off his hood, Max had to squint until his eyes adjusted. They had taken him to a hunting cabin. Like most cabins, this one consisted of a large main room with kitchenette attached and a small hall leading to a bathroom and bedrooms. Deer heads had been mounted on the wooden walls. An old stone fireplace, heavy with soot, stood off to the right. A loft with enough room for a twin bed hung over the kitchenette.

As Max noted the sound of a van driving away, he counted three men plus Leon. Two of them sat on one of three couches lining the walls. Another man worked at a small desk near a back door leading outside. The ceiling opened all the way to the roof, complete with exposed beams and cross braces. And in the center of the room, dragging a simple wood chair over, casual yet full of tension in his tight grip — Leon.

Summoning a calm, cool, and in control persona — one that Max did not think he would find within — he sighed and said, "Do you really need to tie me up? I met you willingly. I'm here to talk."

Leon sat. He made no effort to appear relaxed, no effort to fake friendship. "You met me in High Point to talk. You did not come here willingly, so let's knock off the bull."

"However you want to handle this. Though I'd prefer the *no torture* version."

"Nobody wants to harm you."

"My current situation is not inspiring a lot of confidence in what you're saying."

"You wanted the truth, the answers, the full story of what's going on here. Well, I'm going to tell you. Because you're wrong about a lot."

"Maybe I don't need to know. I'm starting to get the feeling that knowing too much might be like seeing the face of a kidnapper. Not that you're a kidnapper—I'm not a kid, for one thing, and I already know what you look like. But the full story, I don't really need that. I could be fine—"

Leon put his heavy grip on Max's knees. "Be quiet."

Max stopped babbling.

"I'm sure you have spent plenty of time with the Mobley Coven to have heard their fiction about all of this. Let me tell you what really happened. Early in her life, Mother Hope became well-known amongst witches. She was powerful and moral — two traits not often associated together. She wanted to use witchcraft to help people, not control them. From early on, she recognized the threat that the Hulls brought to North Carolina, and she wanted to stop them. Of course, that would take nearly a century to accomplish, but I want you to see that from the start, she thought about doing good, doing right with her gifts."

"What about all that *greed* talk?"

"Eunice Mobley. She had a lot of greed within her bones. It

metastasized in her soul, rotting her bones and spoiling her mind. She knew about Mother Hope, of course, and had reached out on several occasions. But Mother Hope showed no interest."

"Until the deal was struck. When Eunice Mobley began her coven." Max hated to admit it, but even this little bit cast the coven's story into a new light.

"Yes. That was the point that Mother Hope decided to befriend Eunice in an attempt to guide the rising witch along a better path. But Eunice had been trying for years to form a coven. It never lasted."

Max thought of the photos he had seen — Eunice standing with a group of girls.

"I see it on your face," Leon said. "You know about those covens."

"I didn't know they were covens."

"Technically, they weren't. Merely attempts to start such a thing. But she was too young to rally girls who would be serious about it. Those that gravitated towards her were looking for thrills or being silly or trying to make a fool out of the strange Eunice Mobley."

Another thought sent shockwaves through Max. "The girl with the eyes."

"Eunice thought she had a real disciple with that girl. Even after she formed a successful coven, the girl with the eyes seemed to follow along. But it didn't last. Mother Hope convinced the girl to leave the coven. Too late, I'm afraid. Eunice murdered her. There's never been a body recovered or enough evidence to arrest her.

"But we're off the main story. Eunice cut her deal and formed her coven, and she wanted Mother Hope to join, as a way to increase the strength of the coven as well as its notoriety. That's what destroyed any possible alliance between them. Eunice Mobley's thirst for power consumes her. She is blind to all else. I've seen covens before. They tend to behave much like a true sorority — a group of women bonding into sisterhood, working together, helping each other, but always living their own lives, growing through life on their own. The Mobley Coven is more of a cult. Those women live and die for Eunice Mobley. She is everything to them."

Max couldn't deny Leon's words. They sounded more truthful than most anything he had heard regarding this case. A thought struck Max. "You've been keeping a watch on them. For decades, probably."

"Only an idiot allows his enemies to go about unchecked. Especially on home turf."

"But why keep all of this secret from Mother Hope? Why not tell her and use all the resources of the Magi?"

Leon looked around at the Goodman hunters, then angled in even closer. In a soft voice, he said, "I am protecting her. Just like the President, I'm giving her plausible deniability."

"Protecting her from who?"

"Until now, she has made sure that Eunice and her cult remained quiet, unnoticed. They gained power, but we kept a close eye on them. If Mother Hope found out what the Mobley Coven was up to, that they were making a play for her power, she would have been forced to destroy them. That would send a terrible message to all the other covens and witches. It might even push Mother Hope over a mental cliff. I told you before that things were unstable at the moment. Well, this kind of thing can turn a good, moral woman like her into a monster like the Hulls."

Max put more pieces together. "If it all looks like it's the doing of the Goodman hunters, then she can remain on the right side of the moral equation."

"Now, you see."

"I do." Max winced as he said, "But I have to ask you — why are you doing this to me? All that you've done protects Mother Hope except this. I'm on retainer for her — both financially and as a result of the curse. Why not just tell me all of this at the bus terminal?"

"You know why. You stole the last brick."

Max figured as much. "So, now what? You think you can use me as a bargaining chip?"

"Not with the coven. Sandra would trade the brick for you in a second, but the coven will never give up that brick. Even after we grab one of their witches and destroy her along with the brick we have, they won't ever give up that last brick. Doing so means killing Eunice, and they're too brainwashed to let that happen."

"Then what?"

Leon sat back and rubbed his face. "That's what I have to figure out. You might as well get comfortable. You're not going anywhere."

Chapter 31

FOR SEVERAL HOURS, Max remained bound in his chair. Leon left, taking all but Grant Felder with him, and Grant had worked quietly at his desk the entire time since. Max had tried to sleep — a better choice than panic — but his wrists chaffed at the ropes and the burns kept him awake.

"I need to use the bathroom," he said, startling Grant from a laptop. Though he mostly wanted to get up and move around, Max did need the bathroom, too — it had been at least three hours since they abducted him, and possibly longer.

"Hold it," Grant said.

"Then you better get my mind off of it, or there'll be a mess to clean up."

"Don't you dare."

"Talk with me, then. Distract me. Tell me how you got involved with all of this. Frankly, what you're doing doesn't make much sense — I mean, you specifically."

That caught his attention. "What're you talking about?"

"You working with Leon. I completely understand why you would want to reform the Goodman hunters. When I first learned about witches, that they were real and all, I felt the same way. It's scary knowing there are people who can wield such power. That's dangerous. So, I get it. Plus, you've got a family legacy backing you, both with money and the knowledge of what you're doing. But Leon — he works directly for Mother Hope. Why would you align yourself with a guy who works for a witch? Look at that tattoo on your arm. I know what it can do. Why would you let him do that to you and others? That's witchcraft. Not to mention the way you're killing these witches — using spells to find them and spells to destroy them. Doesn't that seem wrong?"

"We're fighting fire with fire."

"I'm not so sure that makes sense with witchcraft."

"It's better than letting the witches take over the world."

"Ah, I get it. You're the unsung heroes, the real deal, not looking for glory or fortune. You just want to save humanity. Is that it?"

"Shut up," Grant said, returning to his laptop.

"If you're not going to talk with me, then you better get me to a bathroom."

"Keep your mouth and your bladder shut. This cabin's been in the Felder family for four generations. You ruin that floor and I'll ruin you."

"You'd better help me out, then. Urine stink is not something you'll get out of wood once it's stuck in there."

Grumbling, Grant pulled a .38 revolver from the desk drawer and walked over. He put the gun to Max's head before he untied the ropes. "Don't try anything."

Gingerly rubbing his wrists, Max went down the hall. Grant followed him, the gun always aimed and ready, and pointed to the bathroom door. After Max relieved himself — and it turned out to be a great relief, far more needed than he had realized — he went back to his chair. The entire time, he searched for an escape.

"You don't really need to tie me up again. Where am I going to go? I don't even know what part of the state I'm in. For that matter, we could be in Virginia for all I know."

"Could be. Could be we're in South Carolina. Or Tennessee. Or maybe we drove you around in circles and we're only blocks away from the High Point terminal."

Grant paused and frowned. Max opened his mouth to ask what was the problem, but before he spoke, he understood — it had been easy for Grant to untie Max. He had a gun and Max was tied to a chair. But getting Max tied up again would be a different matter.

They locked eyes. In that fraction of a second, Max recalled what Bill Corte had said about Grant Felder — a mediocre card shark who wanted to sit in the back and let the rest of the hunters do the ugly work. Max noticed Grant's limp hold on the .38, and how the man's top lip beaded with sweat.

Calculated risk or hunch — Max didn't care about the label. As the next second ticked by, he acted. Lurching forward, he knocked Grant's gun hand aside and sent an elbow upward. A satisfying grunt followed as he smashed Grant's chin.

The gun clunked on the floor, but Max had no time to scrabble for it. He kept his focus on his enemy. While his technique would draw a frown and a headshake from his instructors, his muscles remembered all the lessons the black belts had taught him. It didn't matter how pretty or precise his form looked. Not at that moment. All that mattered was landing blow upon blow, overwhelming Grant with a non-stop flurry of fists that drove that man backwards.

Grant's foot caught on the edge of the desk leg. He crashed to the floor. Blood covered his nose and mouth as he rolled into a fetal position.

"Stay there," Max said. He relaxed his fists as dull aches pulsed along his knuckles. When he felt certain that Grant would not move, he went to retrieve the gun. Stepping backwards, always keeping his eyes on his opponent, he inched his way until he saw the weapon off to his left. As insurance, Max said, "You make a move, and I'm going to kill you."

"Funny," Leon said from behind him, "I was about to say the same thing."

Max's heart dropped as he raised his hands.

"Turn around. Slowly."

Max complied. In the front doorway, he saw Leon holding a handgun. His Goodman hunter goons stood behind him. At his side stood a young woman with her hands bound. She had a blond ponytail, black nails, and a crooked smile — Jessica Mobley.

Chapter 32

WHILE TWO MEN HUDDLED OVER GRANT, sitting him by the desk and treating his wounds, Jessica and Max were tied to two chairs and backed against a wall. Leon and two more Goodman hunters went to one of the bedrooms down the hall. Max heard Leon conferring and giving orders — presumably on the phone since nobody left the bedroom in a rush to follow commands.

"What happened?" he whispered to Jessica.

She sat upright, displaying the firmest posture Max had ever seen and her stiffness carried through to the rest of her behavior. Even as she spoke with Max, her voice naturally soft, she maintained her straight back and alert eyes. This odd demeanor unnerved him.

Until he heard what she had to say.

"After you disappeared, your wife became quite demanding."

"I'll bet."

"We implemented a new plan. I allowed myself to be caught so that your ghost could follow me. Apparently, he was once a detective and had the necessary skills to succeed."

Max looked around the room. "Where is he?"

"How should I know? I don't see ghosts. I'm sure he'll be here soon."

"Relax," Drummond said. "I'm here already. Just wanted to spy on Leon for a moment, get an idea where things stand."

Max fought the urge to cheer. "Good to see you, partner."

"I take it," Jessica said, "that your ghost as arrived."

"He's here."

"Tell him to get back to the coven and hurry."

Drummond said, "On my way."

Max wanted to tell him to wait, to ask what was going on,

but clearly they had a plan in motion and he would have to be patient. He looked back at Jessica, and it hit him why she bothered him — *this was not the way she had behaved when they first met.* Not even close. And the longer he watched her, the more he saw her fear trembling right beneath the surface.

"Has something gone wrong?" he asked.

"Shh. I have to prepare. In case ... in case the spell doesn't last much longer."

"What spell?"

"Be quiet."

She closed her eyes. Perhaps meditating before casting a spell. Whatever the case, she wouldn't be helping Max anytime soon. But Drummond would. He was out there, getting to Sandra so that they both could do something to help. That gave Max more than a little comfort.

Leon and his two cohorts stomped back into the room. The other Goodman hunters perked up, watching Leon like dogs eager to please their Alpha. The two that followed him broke off to either side. One of them stepped out through the front door. The other took the back exit.

"I can't be here when you begin the process," he said to his men. "We all must answer to somebody, and my boss would not be happy if I was found here."

Max nearly laughed. Not happy? Leon's understatement did not come close to painting the picture of Mother Hope disemboweling him for doing all of this behind her back.

"Is he going to be okay?" Leon asked.

One of the men nodded. "Broke his nose and gave him a lot of bruises. He'll be fine."

"Good." Leon stepped toward the desk, and his men cleared the way, leaving Grant Felder to cower. Leon put out his hand, and as if by a witch's spell, one of the men that had gone outside returned with a satchel. He set the handles into Leon's grip and took three steps back. "You'll need this." From the satchel, he pulled out a red brick and set it on the desk. "Call me when it's done."

Outside, a car's engine turned over and idled. Leon snapped

a finger at his man and the two walked out of the cabin, a bit too much like members of the Gestapo for comfort. The front door slammed shut with a finality that jolted Max's nerves. And he had thought his nerves had nothing left in them.

All the men stared at the door as if they expected Leon to return with more orders. They probably would have stayed that way, but Grant stood, holding an icepack to his nose, and said with a nasal tone, "You all know what you should be doing, so get to it."

With a touch of orchestrated chaos, the men jumped into action. Two of them cleared the floor in front of Max and Jessica. Another brought a ladder from outside. The fourth climbed up with a drill in hand and installed a pulley to the top of one of the exposed beams.

Once that job had been completed, the man threaded a thick rope over the beam and through the pulley. He dropped down and removed the ladder. The other men returned with brooms and swept the floor. Finally, the man with the drill had exchanged it for some chalk. He drew a large circle with the rope falling at the center.

Throughout it all, Max checked on Jessica. She watched without outward emotion. Even when two of the men stepped outside, only to return with a round metal tub. Even when they set it in the circle and cast lewd gazes upon her. Even when they attached a hose to the kitchenette sink and filled the tub with water. She never twitched or flinched. Her breathing remained steady. A rock could not be as stoic.

After they filled the tub, they removed the hose, and one man faced Grant Felder. "It's all ready."

Grant set his icepack on the table and picked up the brick. He approached with deliberate steps. As he walked by the tub and the rope and the circle, he inspected the work with a casual glance. Then he lowered between Max and Jessica. He placed a hand on her knee.

"It's a shame to see a girl as young as you caught up in all of this," he said, his voice fuller than before. She looked straight ahead as if nothing existed — not the cabin, not the tub of water, and certainly not Grant. Attempting to shirk off the insult, he went on, "You should be at college. You should be going on dates and to dances and whatever your generation does for fun. But a witch coven? You don't belong in that mess."

He lifted the brick into her line of sight. Max thought he saw a spark of interest, but she did her best to hide any expression.

"I'm sure you know what this is — who this is." Grant grabbed her chin and forced her to look at him. "It's not you. Your spirit is not in this brick. So why would allow yourself to die for it? Loyalty is only valuable if the person you are loyal to appreciates what you do. Otherwise, it makes no difference to the outcome of things. People don't like to admit that, but it's true. They want to hold onto this noble idea that loyalty in itself is valuable. That's nonsense. Think about that. You have a chance to free yourself. Right now. Unlike most witches throughout history, I'm willing to give you a choice. A chance to save your soul. All you have to do is renounce this wicked way of life and tell us where the other brick is. Simple, really. Do that, and you won't be harmed. You won't have to feel the excruciating pain. You won't have to die." He let her chin free and she immediately returned to staring out at nothing. "Please. I have no desire to kill a young woman."

Part of Max wanted to shout at her, to tell her to do as Grant said, to demand that she free herself from a terrible death. He had seen enough witches go through this, and he did not want to see it again. But another part of him knew she had to take her stand. Just because other people were scared of witchcraft shouldn't mean that she had to shy away from it. And most important, Max had to believe that this was all part of some plan, that Sandra and the coven worked furiously to achieve some spell, curse, or other kind of magic.

We just have to hold out long enough.

"Last chance," Grant said. "I'll give you ten seconds to decide."

And he waited. Max watched as Grant stared at Jessica and

Jessica stared at nothing. The Goodman hunters all stood silent, each one ready to act once Grant gave the command. Max could see the honest hope in Grant's eyes — he desperately wanted this young women to absolve him of the dark things he had prepared to do. Up until this moment, he had avoided getting his hands too dirty, but now, Leon Moore demanded he be the one to carry out a murder. He needed her to save herself. It was the only way out for him.

But Max also saw the grim acceptance come over his face as the final seconds drifted by. Even before they had reached the end, everybody knew she would not acquiesce. Of the men standing a few feet back, Max counted two that were excited to torture and destroy a witch. The other two looked unenthusiastic. They had a job to do, one that must be done or else they would suffer a terrible fate. Beyond that, Max couldn't tell — perhaps they were disgusted, perhaps they were apathetic, or perhaps they were simply better at hiding their bloodlust.

Grant lowered his eyes. "You sure you want to die for that old hag?"

As if drugged, Jessica lolled her head at Grant. A mad smile brightened her eyes. "You're the one that's going to die."

Turning away, Grant looked towards Max as if to say *You saw that I tried to save her.* He snapped his fingers and his men came forth. They grabbed the rope hanging from the rafters and pulled it until they had more than they needed.

"Salt the water," Grant said, and one man hustled to the kitchenette, grabbed a container of salt, and dumped all of it into the tub. By the time he had finished, the men with the rope had freed her from the chair, wrapped the rope several times around her ankles and calves, and tied her hands behind her back.

Jessica looked up at Max. "Be ready," she said.

Before he could respond, the Goodman hunters hauled on the other end of the rope, sweeping her feet out from under her, and stringing her upside down over the tub of salted water. Without pausing, they lowered her head into the water. She held still for a long time, but they waited her out. Soon her body craved air. She thrashed and wriggled, and on Grant's command they pulled her up sputtering, gasping, and coughing.

But Max saw in her eyes, the same dull glaze from before. *She's under a spell.* Of course. They sent her to get caught knowing what that meant — torture and possible death. They must have cast a spell for her or maybe created some cocktail that numbed her to all the pain.

Which meant it was up to Max now. She could endure the assault, but she would be too numb to think her way through this. Drummond must have told the coven where the Goodman hunters had taken Jessica, so Max only had to buy them time.

He could do that.

Chapter 33

THERE WERE FOUR GOODMAN HUNTERS PLUS GRANT. They all wore the same black outfits and moved with the same tough-guy swagger. But little things differentiated them, and Max focused on those aspects to tell them apart — Glasses, Paunch, Twitch, and No-Neck.

Paunch and No-Neck manned the rope. They kept Jessica suspended in the air or plunged underwater depending on Grant's orders. Glasses sat on the couch by the back wall while Twitch leaned on the couch's arm.

"Look at what you're doing," Max said, directing all of his words towards Grant. "This is an innocent woman. You really think you'll get away with it?"

Grant put out his hand to halt Paunch and No-Neck from dunking Jessica once more. "Don't go down that road. If you start threatening to blab, then you'll put us in an unfortunate position."

"You're really going to threaten killing me? Like that wasn't already part of your plan."

"It's not. Still isn't."

"I see. You plan to torture and murder this girl and then let me go free. Sure, I'll believe that."

"She's not a girl. She's a witch!" The words spit out of Grant. "That's why this isn't murder. You can only murder a human being, and a witch has given away what makes her human. She is an abomination."

"I get what you're saying, but the police and the courts and the juries won't see any of that. They don't know that witches are real, that magic is real. All they're going to see is a group of people with delusions of the supernatural that went on a murder spree. There's a good chance, though, that you'll do your time in a mental hospital."

"I am not crazy."

Keeping his voice calm, Max said, "I know that. I'm simply telling you how the public will view things. It's not like you've done a good job hiding the evidence. We found the women you kidnapped — at least, what was left of them."

"That's right," Grant said moving around the tub so he faced Max closer. "And yet here we are. You didn't turn us in. Neither did the coven. They don't want the police involved at all, and neither do we. That's always the way it's been. Witches prize their privacy — even when it comes to things like this. Perhaps *especially* when it comes to things like this. That's why I'm not afraid of the police. They'll never know any of this happened. And as long as you don't get stupid, you'll be let go because you won't have any evidence on you. No body, no brick, no crime at all. In fact, if you try to file a report, all you can do is tell them about witches and curses and spells, and you'll get yourself locked away in a mental hospital."

Max refrained from saying more. Guilt, fear, and anger rolled together in Grant's eyes, and Max thought if he pushed the man any harder, the backlash might get Jessica killed. As Grant stepped back towards the desk, Max wished for Drummond to appear with a Hail Mary or any plan. But he did not arrive.

That meant the coven needed more time. Max may have pushed Grant close to the edge, but that weak man wasn't the only one in the room. No-Neck and Paunch wouldn't listen to him. They held the rope to a witch's life. That was too heady, too much power in their hands, for them to listen.

"How about you?" Max called across the room. He purposely did not direct his question to either Glasses or Twitch — whichever one responded would be the one open to talk.

Twitch — a repetitive spasm near his eye — popped to his feet. "Shut up, man."

"You really willing to go to jail for all of this?"

"I'm willing to do a hell of a lot — like punch your face in."

Twitch peered over at Grant for approval.

"Can't do anything without Grant's okay, huh?"

Twitch involuntarily rubbed the back of his hand — the one with the flaming cross tattoo.

"Forget it," Max said. He did not want to be Grant's excuse for burning Twitch to ash. "I'm sorry. I'm sure all of you can understand that I'm a bit frazzled by all of this."

With an amused nod, Grant said, "Come on, now, Mr. Porter. You want to try to convince my followers to betray me? You go right ahead. Let's see what you can do."

All of the Goodman hunters stared at Max. Though he kept his focus on Grant, he could feel them watching him, wondering how he might step up to the challenge, and waiting for the word so they could pounce on him. His muscles ached in expectation of the beating they would put him through.

Come on, Sandra. Drummond, come tell me it's all okay. They were both such strong people, and he wanted them by his side. Things always worked better when he knew they were right there, ready to help him out. Of course, they were helping. But knowing Sandra sat in a casting circle in an attic with a bunch of witches did not make his current predicament any easier. He needed strength to fight these bullies and ...

A nasty smile rose to his lips."You know what really pisses me off?" Max's words took the men by surprise. They shifted their eyes towards Grant like spectators at a tennis tournament. "People like you. You're so condescending. You stand there and act all tough and powerful like you're so much better than a hard-working guy. But you only act that way because I'm tied up. You're not tough."

Grant smirked. "That's going to be your grand strategy? Mocking me?"

"I don't have to mock you. You're a mockery of yourself. These guys know it, too. The reason they follow you — the only reason they obey anything out of your weak little mouth — is that they've got that curse tattooed into them. You were tasked with buying their loyalty, but you couldn't even handle that, so you had to curse them. They don't respect you or fear you. They fear the tattoo."

Though Grant kept a stern face, his eyes darted from man to man. No-Neck avoided Grant's gaze by watching Jessica as he readjusted his grip on the rope. Glasses stared at the floor while Twitch took a sudden interest in the wall paneling. Only Paunch met Grant's eyes, but Max couldn't get a read on what went between the two.

Max braced himself for the punches to come, but instead, Grant returned to the desk. From one of the drawers, he produced a hunting knife. "You can say whatever you want. It won't change anything. We have a job to do. We have to protect the world from these witches, and that's what we're going to do."

"That's right. You're the witch hunters that use witchcraft." Max shot a direct look at Paunch. "I don't know what he's told you about witchcraft, but the stuff is dangerous to mess with. It's like cocaine or heroin. Highly addictive. Why do you think all these sweet women end up witch hags?"

Paunch's eye twitched. "I ain't no woman."

"Works on men, too. I've seen it."

Grant pointed the knife at Paunch. "Don't talk to him. Don't even look at him."

"I ain't your puppet." To Max, Paunch asked, "What are you talking about?"

"Look at what you're doing. Casting spells to destroy witches is using magic."

"And it works." Grant raised the brick in one hand and the knife in the other. "With this witch eliminated, we'll only have one more and our task will be complete. The head of the coven will be destroyed which will free the rest of the women from her evil hold."

"Sure," Max said, shaking his head. "It doesn't work like that. If it did, there would only be a handful of witches left in the world."

From the concern on Paunch's face, Max thought he might be getting through to the man. That would be all the stalling he would need. Paunch's doubts would take over, cause the men to argue, and Max could sit back and wait.

But Grant must have caught on as well, for he blustered over to Paunch. "This man is a devil. You cannot believe his lies. He defends a witch. He works for a witch coven. What part of that makes you think you should trust him?"

No-Neck said, "Can we all shut up and get this over with? My arms are getting tired."

Paunch hesitated.

Grant said, "We all bear the tattoo. If you don't want to do this because you fear what might happen in the long run, stop worrying. Our failure will mean a fiery death in the short run. There won't be a long run to fear and worry about."

With the face of a scolded child, Paunch reset his grip on the rope. "Shut up and get carving. We don't want to be here all night."

Grant turned away, but not before shooting a triumphant glare at Max. He then stooped over to bring his face close to Jessica. Waving the brick in front of her, he said, "You had your chance. I'd pray for your soul, but you're going to a dark, violent place by your own free will."

She spit at him and started laughing – a shrill cackle that belonged with an older, heftier, and more frightening visage. "You're too late," she said.

The lights went out.

The dark lasted only a second, but in that short time Max heard the splash of Jessica hitting the water when Paunch and No-Neck let go of the rope, he saw the pale glow of Drummond appear only a few feet away, and he heard the startled gasps of the Goodman hunters.

The lights flicked back on.

And those gasps turned into terrified shrieks.

Four of the coven witches stood in the cabin – one behind each of the men except for Grant. They wore flowing cloaks and resembled nothing like the cloister of gentle yet odd women Max had seen in that quaint, suburban home. These women each looked like a version of Grandma Mobley harboring only traces of the women they were before. With translucent skin, emaciated faces, bulging eyes, and glimmers of hatred, they hissed in unison like angry snakes. And they attacked.

Glasses tried to stand but the witch next to him spread her fingers into claws and sunk them into his neck. She ripped back and blood sprayed over her. Laughing she turned toward Twitch.

His witch held him from behind in a bear hug. Astonished that such a frail-looking woman could be so powerful, Max watched as Twitch lost control of his bladder. A series of snaps like firecrackers went off and Twitch dropped to the ground. No more than a stuffed doll empty of bones.

Drummond swept across the room and hovered near Max. "Don't worry. They won't bother you."

"Is that what they're doing? *Bothering people?*"

No-Neck and Paunch inched toward the front door, standing back to back as they moved. Three witches encircled the men, taunting and jeering as they reached out. The men swatted at the hands to the delight of the witches, that taut mixture of adrenaline and fear palpable in the air.

"Go away!" Grant cried out.

Max spotted him cowering at the back door. It appeared that Grant had attempted to sneak out the back, but the witch with blood dripping from her clawed hand stood in his way. He clutched the brick in both hands, holding it out like a shield.

"B-B-Begone!"

The blood-stained witch chortled as she loomed closer. A veined and blistered tongue poked out as she licked her lips. Max tried to picture one of the women that stood in the back of the Mobley Coven's house, tried to understand what magic had done to them, but he could not bring the two images together.

Jessica, however, knew better. She came up behind Grant. Her clothes, hair, and face dripped water on the wood floors. Aping Grant's earlier tone, she stooped over him and said, "It's a shame a young boy like you is caught up in all of this. You should be in college. Not out here getting yourself ripped to shreds over what? A bunch of women who know more about how to access the world's energy than you've ever thought possible? That's foolish."

Grant gazed up at her, and Max saw the shift in his eyes. There would be no escape, no reprieve, nothing but death. And at that exact moment, Max knew that Grant had the strength to die on his own terms.

"Leon Moore! Leon Moore! He's our leader!" The words spewed from Grant, ever faster, as he dropped the brick and stared at Jessica.

Confused, she said, "Shut up or I'll make your death slow and painful."

"I betray Leon Moore! He's behind all of this!"

No-Neck and Paunch, still stuck at the front door, dropped all sense of threat from their body. In the space of a heartbeat, they looked over at Grant. Paunch whimpered.

And the fires began.

All five of the Goodman hunters, living and dead, burst into flames. They screamed as their skin ignited from the inside. Dropping to the floor, they writhed and bellowed. Sparks showered up into the air. The witches backed away, their twisted gaze fascinated by the fires. Soon the men's faces and forms became darkened shapes, then darker ash, until they fell apart and burned into nothing.

No physical trace remained.

Only the faint odor of burning.

Jessica picked up the brick from the floor. "Thank you, my sisters."

The crazed witches congregated near the back door. They shuffled like elderly women in need of walkers. Jessica opened the door and the witches filed outside.

"What about me?" Max said.

Drummond said, "Don't worry. Worse comes to worst, I'll take the pain and cut you free myself."

Over her shoulder, Jessica said, "I must guide my sisters into the woods. They'll be safer there until the spell wears off and they return to normal. I'll be back to get you out."

After she left, Max waited in the silent cabin. Despite all he had witnessed in his life, he still had trouble accepting what had happened. Drummond must have sensed Max's state of mind. "Witches. I'm telling you, pal, no good ever comes from dealing with witches."

"I don't know," Max said. "They just saved my life."

"By killing off five men."

"Actually it was Leon Moore's curse that killed those men. I'm not saying I'm pro-witch, and I'm no idiot — they only are helping me because they need our help. But maybe it's possible for them to have some good inside. Maybe a person doesn't have to succumb to the ugly darkness of it all."

"I get the feeling you're not talking about the Mobley witches."

Jessica returned and cut Max loose. She looked different. No longer the quiet and odd girl he first met. "My sisters need a little time. After that, I'll get them back to the house and into the casting circle."

"Why?" Max said. "You've got the brick, and the Goodman hunters are dead."

"That was our improvised plan because you were taken by them. We still have the original plan to finish."

"Leon Moore?"

Jessica nodded and made a call on her cell phone. His wrists burned and his back ached, but standing free felt wonderful. While Jessica spoke in murmured tones, Max checked over the desk Grant had worked at – nothing stood out.

"You know Sandra will be fine," Drummond said. "It's not like she ever sought this out, that she wants to be a witch."

"*Want* has nothing to do with it. There's a greed that comes with power and money."

"Maybe. But I've also heard people say that it's not that money and power corrupt but rather that money and power accentuate yourself. If you're a kind, giving person, then you use your money and power to do kind, giving things. It's the darkness in people that corrupts them. The money and power only makes their corruption possible."

As Max considered that hopeful idea, Jessica ended her call. "Lena cast a location spell. We know where Leon is."

Max shut the desk drawer. "Then let's go."

Chapter 34

THE DRIVE BACK TO WINSTON-SALEM had a surreal quality. At fifty minutes past midnight, Max expected the usual way life took on a different sensation so late – different sounds, different smells, even a different feel in the air – but this time he barely noticed those things. Instead, he kept picturing those men erupting into human infernos. He kept hearing their pained cries melding with the joyous exaltation of the witches. And the few moments he found the will to shove those thoughts away, the void in his mind filled with what might await him.

He parked in the faculty lot at Wake Forest University's biology department, climbed the stairs, and followed the concrete and brick paths leading to the Z. Smith Reynolds Library. Of course Leon would be here.

Drummond had been polite enough to stay quiet through the drive. He popped in and out of the car in order to check in with Sandra and the coven. Floating next to Max, the two approached one of the side door entrances.

"You sure you don't want me to come along?" the ghost asked.

"You can't do anything in there. Leon knows about you. He always protects himself with wards against you."

"I can still cause a lot of trouble for him."

With a bitter grin, Max said, "I appreciate the thought, but you heard Jessica. We're back to the original plan. You let me know when I can make my move."

"I don't like it."

"You don't like any of it."

"Yeah, but this is worse. Leon has to know you're coming."

Max tried the door and it opened. "He definitely knows I'm

coming. Go to the coven. Make sure they're ready fast. I don't want to have to wait a second longer than necessary."

"You got it." Though he still looked dubious, Drummond vanished.

Max entered the library with a lump in his throat. Like the night itself, the library took on a different sheen after hours. This Mecca of knowledge, this respite from the world, this place of peace and rumination that gave Max so many endless hours of comfort had transformed into an ominous maze of book stacks and twisting halls. His footsteps clicked and died in the odd architecture of the building.

As he walked onto the main floor, he found Leon sitting at one of the research tables beneath the skylights. A dim moon cast the walls in pale light. The man had a bottle of Jack Daniels in one hand while the other massaged his bald head. A single, large candle burned in front of him and a salt circle had been drawn around the table.

"You come here to kill me?" Leon said, lifting his bleary eyes.

Max stopped at the edge of the circle. "I don't kill people."

"After what you've done, being dead is the better alternative for me."

"You did this to yourself. Going behind Mother Hope's back. Stupid. You had to have known this would never end well. Even if you got away with it, Mother Hope would eventually find out. Even if you found some way to tell her, let her know that your intentions were to protect her, concoct some crap that she might believe, she would still punish you."

Leon shrugged. "I don't live in *what-ifs*. The witches got the bricks now, and those men are all dead by magic. Mother Hope will know soon enough because I guarantee you Eunice Mobley's going to be coming back with a vengeance." He peeked over at Max's feet. "Come on and have a seat. You can enter the circle. It's only there to protect me from your ghost."

Max weighed his options and decided to walk to the edge of the desk but not sit down – he needed room to maneuver when Drummond gave the word. "Tell me something – do you really believe in Mother Hope, the Magi, all of that?"

"I do."

"I mean deep inside. Be honest. Did you join up with her because you wanted to help her fight the Hulls and abuses of magic or because she promised to keep you alive, cure you, make you younger, give you some power?"

"I believe in the mission."

"But you abused magic with the Goodman hunters and you let Mother Hope abuse magic by cursing me and making you younger and all of it."

"Can't be perfect."

"You guys aren't anywhere near close. I don't think you all even try."

Leon pushed back from the table and tipped the whiskey bottle over his mouth. He guzzled it for a second, letting some of the brown liquid run down his chin, before pointing a weaving finger at Max. "You didn't come here to kill me and you ain't here to chat. What the hell do you want? You here to gloat? Gonna wait until Mother Hope shows up and shreds my skin from my skull? That it?"

The amulet around Max's neck tingled against his skin. "I'm here because tonight we're changing how things are going to be done from now on."

Leon let out a short burst of laughter, paused to eye Max sideways, then laughed even harder. "You're crazy, you know that?"

"I've been told before."

"After all that's happened, you think there's anything you can say, anything you can threaten me with, that'll change my loyalty to Mother Hope? What do you think I'm doing here tonight? I'm drinking a goodbye to my life because I know, eventually, I'm going to have to face her. Mobley's going to restore her soul, her deal with Mr. Whatever-his-name-is will come due, and she'll turn out another deal, one that involves taking down Mother Hope. It's the only outcome Eunice can shoot for. No matter what, Mother Hope ain't going to like it. I kinda hoped you might be here to kill me, but you're too much of a weakling for that. But get this through your thick-headed book brain – I'd rather endure her worst wrath than betray her for you."

As Leon rambled, Drummond appeared several feet away. He moved forward, halting when he saw the salt circle on the floor.

"Ready?" Max asked.

Drummond flicked his Fedora and nodded. At the same time, Leon snarled his top lip and said, "Give me your best."

Max shot forward, planted his hands on the desk, and vaulted across. His feet swung around and landed on Leon's chest. The large man tumbled backward, out of the circle, and Max followed through, straddling Leon.

Part of Max noted that Drummond watched but did not interfere. Good. That let him focus on Leon.

Max ripped Leon's shirt open.

"What is this? You gonna strip me?" Leon tried to resist, but the whiskey had weakened his responses. He waved his arms around ineffectively.

As an answer, Max yanked out the amulet. It glowed a bright green that bounced off the walls and stacks turning the dark library into an emerald cavern. With each pulse of the light, heat rolled up Max's arm.

Taking a deep breath, he recited the words Sandra had drilled into his head. "One with me. One with my pain. One with all I endure."

Plunging the amulet onto Leon's chest, Max winced as the bright green turned a violent red-orange that shot off in numerous directions with laser precision. Leon writhed beneath the amulet, screeching and crying. Max could smell burning as the amulet grew hotter in his hand. Leon jolted once more, bucking at Max, until he arched back with his eyes wide and motionless like a dead man's last gaze.

Then he collapsed to the floor. The light emitting from the amulet ceased along with the heat it generated.

Panting, Max managed to stand. He let the amulet drop to the floor.

"What did you do to me?" Leon asked, rubbing his chest as he sat up.

"Congratulations. You've now been cursed."

"Huh?"

"With the help of some generous witches and that amulet, I just pulled my first, and hopefully only, curse. It's a lesser curse than the one Mother Hope has inflicted upon me, but nasty nonetheless."

Too drunk and beaten to move, Leon spat at Max's shoes. "I don't care what you did to me. I'll get Mother Hope to break it and then she'll kill you."

"No, that won't happen. See, that curse on you, it ties to the curse on me. If Mother Hope harms me with magic, especially if she enacts the curse she put on me, then all of what happens to me will happen to you. So, if she breaks the curse on you, then she breaks the curse on me."

"Bastard."

"Our fates are sealed together now."

Drummond clapped his hands. "Great job. Now put in the final nail."

Max glared down at Leon. "Here's what's going to happen. Tomorrow, once you're sober, you will return to the Magi and you will not mention any of this. You will continue to work for her, and you will make sure she never harms me. Because if she does, then you get harmed too."

He could see Leon working it out. "That's it? I'm not going to have to spy for you or lie or anything like that? Just make sure she doesn't kill us both?"

"That's it. For now. I'm sure we'll find plenty of ways to help each other."

"So, I don't have to betray her?"

"Not at all. And I'll do what I can to keep your secret regarding this whole mess."

"She'll find out. She always does."

"Then you blame it on me. I'm the one who worked for the coven, after all, and I'm the one who was there when the Goodman hunters were destroyed. She doesn't need to know your involvement at all."

Leon chuckled. "But she'll want to hurt you for that, and I'll have to talk her out of it."

"Now you're getting it. You all might be more powerful than me, but there are ways around people like you. I think this is going to be one of them."

Max turned to leave, but Leon waved his hand around. "The bricks?"

"They belong to the Mobley coven." Max paused and gave it a quick thought. "I doubt we'll ever see those bricks again."

"But you can bet your white ass we'll see those witches again."

"Probably. Like you said — Grandma Mobley will try to free her spirit and circumvent the evil she made her deal with. But I don't think it's going to be all that easy for her." He rubbed his chest. "Curses never are."

"They'll still come after us, cause us trouble."

"But when that happens, I won't be on retainer for them."

As Max left the library, he heard Leon's drunken, bitter laughter.

Chapter 35

BY THE TIME MAX RETURNED HOME, Sandra had paced a trail into the living room carpeting. She rushed over to him, covering him with her kisses and concern, while he attempted to collapse on the couch.

"Did it work? Are you okay?" she asked.

He kissed her with a smile. "How about you? Still my beautiful wife?"

"Always."

"You sure?"

"I've told you all along that I knew I could handle it. And I did."

Neither slept that night. They talked about what had happened for hours, hashing over every detail of what Leon Moore had said, how the witches attacked the cabin, and whether or not the linking curse would be as effective as they hoped. Sandra told him of the strange experience watching the witches cast such difficult spells, the thrilling prickle of energy that floated in the attic, and the frightening power that formed between them all. Though she had been part of it, she also had sensed the danger.

"There's a darkness in that house. Maybe it's in all covens. But I guarantee you, that won't be me. I was there. I felt it all, and I'm telling you, I'm *promising* you, there is nothing seductive about it for me."

She put her head on his shoulder. They let the rest of the night drift by while he stroked her arm and listened to her breathe. If Drummond had appeared, he kept his presence hidden. However, Max suspected he went to the Other to spend time with one of his lady-ghost friends.

When the sun rose, they cleaned up and drove to the office.

After a short rehash with Drummond, they all settled into their normal routines. Mrs. Porter arrived with PB and both had warm smiles for everyone.

"So?" Max asked. "How did it go?"

PB rushed forward. "It's gonna be cool. Jammer J is back in school and having a good time. He's even got a friend and the teacher told us that he's on his way to being a star student."

Sandra said, "And he's okay with you not going?"

"Yeah. He said he'd much rather be in classrooms with different teachers and other kids and stuff. The idea of home schooling and being stuck with one teacher all day isn't for him." PB turned to Mrs. Porter with a sheepish look. "No offense."

"None taken," Mrs. Porter said. "Since nobody else is willing to step up, I'm more than happy to make sure you get a proper education."

"And this means I still have time to work for the Agency. So, what's up today?"

Max never got a chance to answer. His mother pinched PB's arm and said, "Now, hold on there. We had an agreement. School first, then you get to work with Max. Not the other way around and you know it. You've got to learn to honor your word. Otherwise, your word is worthless and there's nothing more important than a man's word. That's your first lesson. You should write that down."

Though he rolled his eyes and grumbled, Max could see the joy on PB's face.

Mrs. Porter nudged PB toward the door. "I thought we would have school here, but clearly this will be too much of a distraction."

"Aw, come on."

"Off we go. My apartment will do just fine."

"But —"

"No *buts*. Once you show a good work ethic, then we'll talk about doing some classes here at the office."

Max chuckled. "Take some advice. Don't argue with her. I tried it for years and she's still the one in charge."

With his head drooping, he walked out the door – an unmistakable bounce in his step. Max waited to make sure PB didn't run back in with some flimsy excuse. Of course, with his mother in charge, neither of the Sandwich Boys would get away with such things.

Max opened his laptop and waved Sandra over. "I've been working on this all morning. I want you to double-check it."

She peered over his shoulder. He had a family attorney website up and had filled out a form to start the process of becoming PB and J's guardians. Sandra's hand tightened on his arm.

"We're really doing this," she said.

"That's what I want to make sure before I send it."

"You have doubts?"

"Not one. But we had gotten to a point where we were okay with never having kids or a family."

"We do have a family now. This'll just make it official."

"That's how I see it, too. Those boys aren't our blood, but I don't see how they can be anything else but our boys."

Sandra squeezed his shoulders. "Send it, hon."

Despite the fluttering in his chest, Max clicked on SEND and watched the screen change to confirm that they had started on a new road of their lives.

"I've got to tell you," Drummond said from the bookshelves, "I'm so glad that we're going back to the way things always are around here. I'm done with this case. Never should have gotten involved in the first place."

Sandra settled in her chair and leaned back. "You got that right. I mean, I'm happy we helped them and I was fascinated by all that I got to see, but it's hard to deal with that many witches. You never know what to believe."

Max raised an eyebrow. "I'm surprised you're sounding so much like Drummond."

"Can't I have mixed emotions?"

"Of course, but every time I tried to get you away from the witches, you got angry with me."

"You know that wasn't about the witches. It was, and still is, about you trusting me. If you had trusted me, you would've known that no matter how far it seemed I was going along with them, I would never let myself go down that road of darkness. My spirit is clear and intact."

Drummond took off his hat and stretched his arms. "Good. I wouldn't have wanted to go hunting for bricks again."

Max walked over to the new rug. "Hon, I want you to know that this fight we've been having is over."

"Oh?" she said with some bite.

"That's right. You think I don't trust you enough, and I've listened to that. I've thought about it, and I know you were dead on. I was worried so much about things I couldn't control that I messed up with the things I can control."

"What is it you control?" More bite, this time with a hint of skepticism.

"Myself. I can control my worry. I can control my fears. I can control my mouth."

Drummond laughed. "Doubt that last one."

"And I can show you that I heard you, that I believe in you, that I trust you."

He reached down and pulled back the rug. Underneath, neatly painted on the floor, he presented a beautiful casting circle. It had thick lines and an inner circle for writing symbols.

Sandra gasped. "Max, it's incredible."

"It should be enough for all the basic spellwork you do. And it has a groove cut along the center of the outer circle for salt or other stuff to be spread safely. Plus, I figure that way nobody can break the salt circle by just sliding their foot across. Everything will remain in the groove. I think you'll find it good for all your studies. You like it?"

She dabbed at her eyes. "This is perfect."

"Be sure to thank PB, too. This is the project I had him working on."

Drummond placed his palm on his chest. "I'll have you know that I kept the secret as well. I mean, Max never told me, but you can't really keep much from me in this office."

"Thank you," Sandra said. "Both of you. And I'll be sure to

thank PB. Maybe I'll bake him a pie or something."

Max faced her. "I'm counting on you, trusting you, to become the first great good witch."

With tears sneaking out of her eyes and a sharp sniffle, she beamed at him. "I love you."

Afterword

Hi folks. Here we are again at the end of another Max Porter book, and you know what that means — time for some truth or fiction answers.

To begin with, George Black was a real man, and his history (as well as the various versions of it) is as true as I can determine. You can find out all about him online and if you're in Winston-Salem, you can visit his home which has been converted into a small museum. Several of the locations that he made the bricks for are real and really do still have his bricks. Notably, the pharmacy and the government building that Max and Drummond investigate. Check them out online and you'll see Black's handiwork, including the lovely brick paths on the sidewalks.

Although the brick warehouse in Thomasville is a real place, to the best of my knowledge Black's bricks were not used in its creation.

Because a few of my early readers wondered, I will fess up here — the Mobley Coven is entirely fictitious as is their long history. While witch covens did, and still do, exist throughout the world, I have not used any specific coven as a basis for those found in my books. Some covens do have websites, which may be of interest to a few readers, but I have no knowledge of darkweb sites catering to witchcraft and covens. I've yet to delve into the darkweb because, y'know, it's dark.

Finally, though the coven is not real, the Greensboro Science Center is. And if you ever have the chance to go, you should. It is a fun, small place that lets you get up-close to a lot of the animals in ways larger zoos and science centers cannot allow. Plus, science is cool and worth supporting.

Acknowledgements

Time for some Thank Yous (my mother taught me well). It's no secret that books are never created only by the author. There are editors, readers, cover designers, and plenty more. Even for an indie author, there will be many people who contribute in ways both big and small to the completion of a book. Some of the names here are regulars, but I'm happy to keep thanking them. Their contributions should never be minimized. This time around, I'd like to thank Ed Schubert, John Hartness, and Gail Z. Martin. Also, for a stunning cover, the incomparable Claudia Ianniciello. As always, my Launch Team never fails me. Thank you so much for testing these books out! And, of course, no book would ever happen without the love and support of my wife and son.

But most of all, I thank you, my readers. Without you, none of this would happen. Plus, you give me the added benefit of being able to tell certain family members *See, it all worked out fine!* I thank you doubly for that!

About the Author

Stuart Jaffe is the madman behind *The Max Porter Paranormal Mysteries,* the *Nathan K* thrillers, *The Parallel Society* series, *The Malja Chronicles, The Bluesman, Founders, Real Magic,* and so much more. His unique brand of old pulp adventure mixed with a contemporary sensibility brings out the best in a variety of SF/F sub-genres. He trained in martial arts for over a decade until a knee injury ended that practice. Now, he plays lead guitar in a local blues band, *The Bootleggers,* and enjoys life on a small farm in rural North Carolina. For those who continue to keep count, the animal list is as follows: one dog, two cats, three aquatic turtles, nine chickens, and a horse. As best as he's been able to manage, Stuart has made sure that the chickens and the horse do not live in the house.

www.ingramcontent.com/pod-product-compliance
Lightning Source LLC
Chambersburg PA
CBHW030520310726
48979CB00010B/1735/J

* 9 7 8 1 9 6 3 5 1 7 0 2 6 *